"What Did You Just Do To Me?" She Demanded In A Low Voice.

"I kissed you."

She shook her head and felt the knot at the nape of her neck give, the heaviness of her hair loosening to tumble down her back. For some reason it signaled a final betrayal, a surrender she neither wanted, nor could avoid. A loss of the worst sort…of herself.

Their kiss couldn't have lasted longer than a moment or two and yet look at what he'd done to her. Or rather, look at how he'd caused her to come undone.

She'd always taken such pride in her cool poise, knowing that others might want, but could never take, not while she held herself at a careful distance.

But with one touch, Gabe had stripped all that away.

Dear Reader,

This will be my final Harlequin Desire title, and I'd like to sincerely thank all the readers who have supported my career and been so encouraging over the years. It's been a true pleasure to share my stories with you and develop relationships with so many who have taken the time to email me. Some of my books have been a direct result of your comments and suggestions.

I would also like to thank Harlequin for seeing something in my first book, *Jinxed,* and helping to launch a career that's spanned so many years. I couldn't have asked for a better first home or better editors to assist me along the way. They have all been fabulous and I thank them all, particularly my current editor, Mary-Theresa Hussey!

I hope you enjoy *Becoming Dante,* part of the ongoing Dante Legacy series. I have to tell you I totally fell in love with Gabe Moretti, one of the forgotten Dantes, who struggles to find his way home and become what he was always meant to be. And I hope you'll look for my next story. I guarantee you'll be delighted with where I take you from here!

Unfortunately, the time has come for me to leave Harlequin, at least for now, but I hope you will continue to follow me and the new books I'm in the process of writing, many with characters and storylines we've both come to love, such as the Dantes.

Please visit my website, www.DayLeclaire.com, where I'll have a list of upcoming releases, along with personal comments and information to keep you in the loop. Do drop by and let me know what you'd like to see from me next.

Love,

Day Leclaire

DAY
LECLAIRE

BECOMING DANTE

HARLEQUIN®

entertain, enrich, inspire™

Recycling programs
for this product may
not exist in your area.

ISBN-13: 978-0-373-73213-5

BECOMING DANTE

Copyright © 2012 by Day Totton Smith

This edition published by arrangement with Harlequin Books S.A.

For questions and comments about the quality of this book, please contact us at CustomerService@Harlequin.com.

® and TM are trademarks of Harlequin Enterprises Limited or its corporate affiliates. Trademarks indicated with ® are registered in the United States Patent and Trademark Office, the Canadian Trade Marks Office and in other countries.

www.Harlequin.com

Printed in U.S.A.

Books by Day Leclaire

Harlequin Desire

*Dante's Honor-Bound
  Husband #2087
  (Gianna and Constantine's story)
Nothing Short of Perfect #2121
More Than Perfect #2139
A Very Private Merger #2162
*Becoming Dante #2200
  (Gabe and Kat's story)

†The Royals
*The Dante Legacy

Silhouette Desire

†The Forbidden Princess #1780
†The Prince's Mistress #1786
†The Royal Wedding Night #1792
The Billionaire's Baby
  Negotiation #1821
*Dante's Blackmailed Bride #1852
  (Severo and Francesca's story)
*Dante's Stolen Wife #1870
  (Marco and Caitlyn's story)
*Dante's Wedding Deception #1880
  (Nicolò and Kiley's story)
*Dante's Contract Marriage #1899
  (Lazzaro and Ariana's story)
Mr. Strictly Business #1921
Inherited: One Child #1953
Lone Star Seduction #1983
*Dante's Ultimate Gamble #2017
  (Luciano and Téa's story)
*Dante's Temporary Fiancée #2037
  (Rafaelo and Larkin's story)
*Dante's Marriage Pact #2057
  (Draco and Shayla's story)
Claimed: The Pregnant
  Heiress #2060

Other titles by this author
available in ebook format.

DAY LECLAIRE

USA TODAY bestselling author Day Leclaire is described by Harlequin Books as "one of our most popular writers ever!" Day's tremendous worldwide popularity has made her a member of Harlequin's "Five Star Club," with sales of well over five million books. She is a three-time winner of both a Colorado Award of Excellence and a Golden Quill Award. She's won *RT Book Reviews* Career Achievement and Love and Laughter Awards, a Holt Medallion and a Booksellers' Best Award. She has also received an impressive ten nominations for the prestigious Romance Writers of America RITA® Award.

Day's romances touch the heart and make you care about her characters as much as she does. In Day's own words, "I adore writing romances, and can't think of a better way to spend each day." For more information, visit Day at her website, www.dayleclaire.com.

To Diana Colpitts,

#1 Dantes fan, and a soul-sister who loves *Star Trek, Star Wars* and NASCAR as much as I do.

Thank you for keeping me entertained
with all your family stories and wild Dante dreams.

Hugs, sweetie!

One

Gabe Moretti's office door slammed open and one of the most beautiful women he'd ever seen swept in. At her appearance, an odd sizzle raced through him, something he'd never experienced before, something that jarred him from complacency and threw all his senses on high alert.

She's yours, came an insidious whisper. *Take the woman!*

Gabe shoved aside the bizarre thought and focused on her, his brows drawing together. She was tall, or rather her three inch heels gave the illusion of height, and emphasized her delicate, almost fragile bone structure. Despite her slender frame, womanly curves filled out a charcoal-and-white suit that could only be Christian Dior. A black wool coat framed the outfit. Hair the color of banked embers fell away from a sculpted face and formed a heavy twist at her nape. But there was more to her than mere beauty. Character and sheer force of will melded with her appearance, while intelligence glittered in eyes a pale, startling green, eyes that were haunting…and haunted. They gave her an almost painful vulnerability, one Gabe reacted to with unsettling intensity.

Get. The. Woman.

The primal demand overcame thought and reason, the visceral tug almost more than he could withstand. Time slowed, stilled, stealing his intellect, his icy control, all that drove him and made him the man he'd fought to become. Desire honed into one imperative…this woman, in this place, captured within this moment. And all the while, the insidious whisper lashed at him. *Take her. Make her yours. Brand her with your touch. Your possession.* Heat crackled, unbearable in its intensity, ungovernable in its strength. It slipped deep inside, infiltrated his veins with each beat of his heart. It took root, sending out endless tendrils that blossomed within his soul. And then time sped up, thrusting him back into the here and now.

The woman checked her forward motion as though sensing some disturbance. She hesitated, her gaze locking with his. Clearly, he wasn't what she'd anticipated and his curiosity grew. Who or what had she been expecting? Or was she simply reacting to him in the same way he reacted to her?

"Gabe Moretti?" she asked in a deep, husky voice that threatened to fry sense and sensibility.

She's the one!

"I'm sorry, Mr. Moretti." His assistant, Sarah, hurried into the office. "She refused to make an appointment and demanded to see you immediately."

Gabe flipped closed the file he'd been reviewing and stood. He pinned the mystery woman with the sort of steely look that had earned him the nickname "Iceman" among both competitors and adversaries. Maybe he reacted so strongly because of the inner voice hammering at him— one he'd never heard before and hoped never to hear again. Or maybe it was to hold instinct at bay, one that insisted he

ignore civilized behavior and take what he wanted, regardless of consequence. She simply returned his look with one
of her own, the expression in her crystalline eyes as brilliant
and fierce as Dante fire diamonds.

Ice versus fire, an intriguing combination.

"Why don't we start at the beginning?" he suggested. It
impressed the hell out of him that he could speak so calmly
while desire fomented within, splashing through him in hot,
messy waves. "Such as, who are you?"

"Don't you recognize me? You should." Amusement fil-
tered through the statement. "I'm Kat Malloy."

The simple statement impacted like a punch to the gut.
So much for some fool, intuitive voice. Not only was this
woman not *the one*, she could *never* be *the one*. No matter
how badly he wanted her on a physical level, she was the
last woman in existence he would take to his bed—or ever
want in his bed. He'd seen her only once before in his entire
life. Even then, he'd felt a similar reaction, though nowhere
near this strong. Perhaps his earlier reaction had been miti-
gated by the fact that she'd been in another man's bed—her
cousin's fiancé's, no less.

Gabe glanced at his assistant and gave a subtle jerk of
his head.

The instant he and Kat were alone, he approached and
delivered the first salvo. "Maybe if you weren't wearing
clothes, I'd have an easier time remembering you."

Irritation flashed through her gaze like emerald lightning.
"How kind of you to bring that up. Ever the gentleman."

"I wouldn't advise going down that road," he said, very,
very gently. "Otherwise I'll be forced to discuss how well
you fit the definition of a lady."

She dismissed his warning with a casual shrug, though
based on the sweep of color darkening her cheekbones, his
comment hit home. Good. So long as he kept their relation-

ship adversarial, it wouldn't allow for any other emotions to creep in—like lust. Or passion. Or the need to rip her clothes off and imprint himself on her, body and soul.

"You've refused every attempt to make an appointment," she said. "The very least you could do is have the courtesy to hear my proposition before throwing me out."

He simply stared at her. Something in his demeanor must have penetrated her annoyance and she stilled, eyeing him warily…a succulent doe scenting a hungry predator. About damn time. He maintained his silence, allowing it to grow until cold, raw bitterness settled between them. And all the while that hideous voice hammered at him, making demands about Kat Malloy he had zero intention of listening to, let alone following.

"I owe you nothing. Maybe my late wife did. After all, you were Jessa's cousin," he said at last. He paused a beat before adding in a conversational tone, "Did you know she loved you like a sister? Even after what you did, even after your little fling with Benson Winters, she still spent the last two years of her life grieving over her lost relationship with you."

"Did she?" Kat raised a sleek eyebrow. "She certainly had a peculiar way of showing it, especially considering she turned our grandmother against me and vilified me in the press. For some reason that just doesn't strike me as very sisterly."

He saw red. "Maybe because you slept with her fiancé. And though I ultimately benefited since she turned to me for consolation, it was a despicable thing to do."

The Malloy woman rallied with impressive speed. "So everyone keeps telling me. For some strange reason, I have a slightly different take on what happened that night."

She gave his office a cursory glance, noting the generous sitting area where he often entertained clients. Ignoring the chairs, she chose the couch. She shrugged off her coat, tossed it over one of the arms and made herself at home, crossing her legs—gorgeous, shapely legs, he couldn't help but notice. Legs he would give almost anything to have wrapped around him. Of course, even a viper had a sinuous shape. That didn't mean he'd get close enough to feel the sting of her fangs or be infected by her poison. Not that his inner voice gave him any peace on that front. Apparently, it didn't care about fangs or poison, only about those legs, and how tight they could hold him.

Regarding him with remarkable self-possession, she said, "Before you throw me out, you should be aware of one vital detail." She smiled her siren's smile. "I have something you want."

He waved that aside. "You have nothing I want, now or ever."

She folded her hands in her lap. So proper. So decorous. So bloody classy. And every bit of it a lie. "Actually, the detail I'm referring to is Heart's Desire."

He froze. *Son of a bitch!* He'd spent years attempting to purchase his mother's fire diamond necklace from Matilda Chatsworth, without success. Kat's grandmother knew damn well how badly he wanted it, that he'd literally do anything necessary to get it back. Granted, not the best negotiating tactics for someone with his skill and experience. But he'd been far younger then, and lacked the ability to maintain a poker face, especially when it came to something that carried so much emotional baggage.

The necklace had been created by his mother, Cara, when she first started working for Dantes as one of their jewelry designers. During those early, heady days, she'd met and fallen in love with Dominic Dante, the owner's son. Their affair had been passionate and all-consuming, teetering on the brink of marriage. But instead of choosing his mother,

Dominic had taken a wife with a bank account balance that would assist Dantes' bottom line, no doubt at the urging of his parents. After his betrayal, his mother had accepted a position at Dantes, New York, and moved on with her life— until Dominic had swooped in years afterward and, unable to resist, she'd indulged in a one-night stand with him. That one night resulted in Gabe's and his twin sister, Lucia's, conception, causing Cara to leave Dantes permanently.

According to Dominic, he'd never forgotten Cara, his love never dying. He spent years attempting to find her, frustrated by how successfully she'd fallen off the grid. Eventually, fifteen years later, he tracked her down, and discovered she'd borne his twins. This time he proposed to her, despite still being married to his wife, Laura. He gave Cara a necklace she'd created for the firm, one he named Heart's Desire in her honor, along with a ring as a promise that he'd come to her after his divorce, marry her and legitimize his bastard twins by adopting them and bestowing the Dante name on them. Of course, that had never happened and all Cara Moretti had been left with were empty promises and the dying flames of the fire diamonds Dominic had given her.

Gabe had been twenty when his mother became ill and, desperate for money to care for her, he'd sold the fire diamond necklace to Matilda Chatsworth. The money had also provided him with a start in life. Despite knowing he'd had no choice but to sell the necklace, he'd always hoped to buy it back. It had taken him a long time to realize why it had become so vital to have it in his possession once again.

Eventually, he'd been able to acknowledge what the necklace represented—the symbolism it held for him, one that continued to burn in his heart. It stood for the man who'd created him. The family that had rejected him. And the mother and sister who had always been there for each other, through the good, the bad and the unbelievably ugly.

Unfortunately, by the time he had the financial where-withal to purchase Heart's Desire, Matilda refused to sell. Even when he'd married her granddaughter Jessa, the neck-lace remained just out of reach, a promise, but never a real-ity. What he didn't get was why, after all these years, had Matilda decided to give her wayward granddaughter the necklace instead of selling it back to him? Why would she turn on him like that, especially when she'd despised Kat for betraying Jessa?

Gabe focused on Kat, aware she'd become an obstacle in his path, one he'd do anything to remove. A blistering fury lapped at his control. "You have it?" Just those three words, but they contained an emotional history that spanned his en-tire life. That went to the very core of who and what he was.

Kat hesitated and answered indirectly. "My grandmother contacted me recently, asked me to return home. She's not well. She promised to give me the necklace after she…" Something painful shifted across her expression before van-ishing. "Afterward."

"In that case, come see me when you actually have it. Now if you don't mind…" He jerked his head toward the door. "I'm busy."

"I'm afraid there's a little more involved than that." She glanced around, her gaze coming to rest on the nearby wet bar and her voice acquired a husky quality. "Is it possible to have some water? I'm dying of thirst."

"Planning to play the role of grieving granddaughter over the impending loss of your grandmother, Kat? Complete with crocodile tears, I have no doubt. Sorry, sweetheart, not buying it."

He caught a flicker of pain before her expression closed over. "Any tears I shed over my grandmother will be real. After my parents died when I was five, Gam raised me. I owe her more than I can ever express. But you don't have to worry about my breaking down in front of you. I never cry. Ever."

Gabe didn't bother to beat around the bush. "How much? How much for Heart's Desire?"

She didn't so much as twitch. "It's not for sale."

He shot to his feet, swearing beneath his breath. "You're a piece of work, you know that? First you sleep with Benson Winters, Jessa's former fiancé. Now you've found a way to wriggle back into Matilda's good graces and get your hands on that necklace. Why? What's your game?"

Her response came just as promptly. "This isn't a game. It never was."

He honed in on the bottom line, at least what he considered the bottom line. "I'll pay you full value for the necklace. More than full value. Money is no object." As usual, when it came to that damn necklace, every business skill and tactic he'd learned over the past decade vanished like mist beneath the rays of a hot summer sun.

"My price isn't money." She waved the discussion aside as though it were of little consequence and offered a cool smile. "I believe you were going to get me a drink?"

Damn, damn, damn. He'd spent no more than five minutes with the woman and she'd already managed to demolish years of effort to curb his emotions, to keep them walled off and under tight control. It had to be because he wanted her. Because she belonged to him. He stiffened in disbelief. Dear God, what the *hell* was happening to him?

Without a word, he crossed to a wet bar. "Flat or sparkling?"

"Flat."

"Ice?"

"Thank you. It would make a nice change."

"That's right." Ice sang against crystal. "You've been hiding out in Europe for the past five years."

"I haven't been hiding," she instantly protested.

Interesting. It would appear he'd managed to hit another hot button. It surprised him that a woman like Kat didn't have her weaknesses better fortified. "Bull. You hightailed it out of the country within days of the news breaking that you were having an affair with your cousin's fiancé, senatorial candidate Benson Winters. And you've stayed out of the country ever since, not even returning when Jessa and I married, let alone for her funeral." He handed her the glass, noting with satisfaction that it trembled ever so slightly in her grasp. "But the minute you figure out how to get your hands on Heart's Desire, you manage to find your way back to Seattle."

She took a quick sip of water, no doubt to give herself a precious few seconds to regain her equilibrium. "Is that why you've repeatedly refused to see me? Because I didn't attend Jessa's funeral?"

"It's as good a reason as any, wouldn't you agree?"

"If it were true." She took another restorative sip, before meeting his gaze. "Which it isn't."

Maybe if he focused on his anger, the desire would go away. Or at least, ease up. That's all he needed, a few minutes of respite from the fierce wave of need lashing at him, eroding his control with every passing second. He didn't understand it. The only emotion he should feel toward her was utter contempt. And yet… That wasn't what he felt. *Why?*

"Which part isn't true?" he bit out. "That you couldn't be bothered to attend your cousin's funeral, or you returned only in order to get your hands on Heart's Desire?"

She gave a careless shrug. "Jessa wouldn't have wanted me there."

"No question about that. And yet the second Matilda tells you she's ill, you return to circle like a vulture. Or am I mistaken about that, as well?"

She flinched, the movement barely perceptible, bringing a hint of vulnerability to those brilliant, haunted eyes. Of course, considering all he knew about her, she'd patented the look and incorporated it into her current scam, something he found far easier to believe than the alternative—that she possessed so much as a modicum of true vulnerability. He couldn't trust his instincts when it came to this woman, not when they urged him to make her his.

A ray of late morning sunshine shafted across the room, losing itself in the trace of red buried in the sooty darkness of her hair. "You're not mistaken. I'm here because my grandmother is ill."

"That's not why you're sitting in my office though, is it?" Cynicism ran rampant through the question. "I believe you're sitting here because you know how much I want Heart's Desire."

Her chin lifted an inch. "You're right. I am. I'm betting you'll do anything and everything to get your hands on it."

"Then name your price."

"I don't want money. What I do want in exchange for the necklace is quite simple and well within your ability to offer me." When he didn't reply, she continued. "I've heard you're one of the best negotiators in all of Seattle. Possibly in the entire Northwest." She set her glass aside and interlaced her fingers, the knuckles blanching white and betraying the nervousness lurking behind her calm façade. "Care to put it to the test?"

"Take your best shot."

"My grandmother is a very traditional woman. Naturally, she's concerned about me, and about my…" She hesitated, before adding delicately, "Shall we say, my unfortunate choices to date? Right now, she isn't open to a reconciliation. She's simply informed me that she intends to honor her promise to give me the necklace and to let me know that's likely to happen sooner rather than later."

"I gather giving you the necklace isn't good enough for you?"

Kat shook her head. "No. I want more. A lot more."

"Your grandmother is a wealthy woman. Let me guess. You feel entitled to a generous portion of that wealth."

She lifted a shoulder in a negligent shrug. "What I want is a reconciliation. My reasons are my own."

"And how do I fit into the picture?"

"Gam has made it clear that she needs proof of my respectability. I believe her exact words were…" She wrinkled her brow in reflection. "'I will need to see for myself that you've settled down with a respectable man who won't put up with any of your nonsense.'"

"Good God," he said faintly.

"Yes, that was my reaction, too. But, if I do what she asks, I believe Gam will welcome me home. That brings me to the aforementioned respectable man." She fixed her spring-green eyes on him and smiled. "Hello, respectable man."

He stared at her, appalled. "You're proposing marriage? No. Absolutely no way. You're insane to think I'd agree."

The flat statement didn't come close to mirroring his profound distaste for her outrageous proposition. Or his profound desire. Marriage. The marital bed. The wedding night. He recalled the first time he'd seen Kat and his hands balled into fists. She'd been nude, sprawled across satin sheets, her youthful face so falsely innocent. Sleeping Beauty well after the prince's "kiss" had wakened her.

Even then, he'd been knocked sideways by her, had felt the initial, confusing stirrings of what had exploded into something far more this time around. He'd assumed all those years ago it had been a natural male response to the sight of a beautiful, naked woman, though he'd never been able to explain why the image of her had been branded into his memory for the past five years, while images of his wife, who died two short years ago, had already faded away. No wonder he hadn't recognized the older, more stylish version of Kat who'd swept into his office. The two couldn't look more different—the buttoned-up sophisticate versus earthy temptation.

She laughed in open amusement. "Relax, Gabe. I'm not proposing marriage. I'm proposing an engagement. Granted, a prolonged engagement. One that will prove to Gam that I've settled down. You'll help make her final months happy ones."

"As if you give a damn about that."

"Actually, I do give a damn. Despite all that's happened, she's still my grandmother." She paused to allow that to sink in, before continuing, "Besides, who could be more perfect? Since you were Jessa's husband, our engagement takes me from infamous to respectable in one easy step. You're renowned for your honor and integrity. For being a powerful man who, though fair, isn't a pushover. You're exactly the man Gam has in mind to…" Her amusement grew, encouraged him to join in on the joke. "To keep me in line."

"No."

"Think of it, Gabe." She used her siren's voice on him, along with those leaf-bright eyes and sultry smile. All of it bent on seduction. "I'll be at your mercy. Forced to toe whatever line you draw. And in exchange, you get your Heart's Desire. Win-win."

He hesitated for a long minute, debating how to handle a proposition he should turn down flat, but found more tempting than he could have believed possible. What was that line from the TV show he'd watched as a child? *Resistance is futile.* He crossed to his desk and pressed a button on his phone. "Sarah?"

"Yes, Mr. Moretti," his assistant said immediately.

"Cancel the rest of my appointments today. I'll be leaving the office and won't be back until the usual time Monday. Reschedule everything for next week. Give the Atkinson project top priority."

He didn't bother waiting for a response. He turned his attention to Kat and gestured toward his office door. "Shall we?"

"Shall we…what?"

Her amusement faded, replaced by a wariness that caused Gabe to smile, though he suspected it lacked any semblance of humor. "Shall we see if we can consummate our future business agreement, of course. Assuming we're able to reach an agreement."

"Consummate," she repeated, stiffening. Nerves jittered across her expressive face. Nerves and something else, something he couldn't quite place. Dread?

He couldn't explain what prompted him to provoke her this way. Perhaps it was that damned vulnerability he'd picked up on, the need to determine whether or not it was just an act. Or maybe he sensed a weakness, something he could exploit in order to gain the upper hand in their battle of wills. More likely it was the lust that had dogged him since the moment she stepped into his office.

He lifted an eyebrow. "Isn't that the end result when a proposal is accepted? The parties consummate the agreement. I suggest we go somewhere more private where we can do so. After all, you've just said that part of the deal was having you at my mercy, forced to toe whatever line I draw. Well, sweetheart, consummating our agreement is my line. So, I suggest you plant the toes of those sexy Valentinos along my line and start begging for mercy."

"You must be joking." She shot to her feet, outrage lacing

her words. Not exactly flattering, considering most women were quite eager to…consummate with him.

Maybe that was why he didn't instantly reassure her. Or maybe it was that damnable inner voice driving him on. Whatever the cause, he gave her another verbal shove. "No, I'm not joking. I am open to conversation beforehand. Perhaps a call to my lawyer to draft something nice and legal so you can't default on our agreement. After that…" He moved in on her, stopping mere inches away. The sizzle between them increased to almost unbearable levels. "Well, let's just say you were right. I'll do whatever it takes to get my hands on that necklace."

"Even bedding me?" The question sounded almost bitter, which roused his curiosity.

"If you insist."

"I don't insist. In fact, I don't want to sleep with you or any other man." Her carefully constructed façade cracked and passionate intensity lashed through her words, increasing his curiosity. "All I want is to satisfy my grandmother's request."

"And all I want is Heart's Desire. You were the one who suggested an engagement as a means to achieve our mutual goals."

"That doesn't mean we have to—" She broke off, her lashes sweeping downward to conceal her expression. One of distaste, if he didn't miss his guess.

"I believe that's something we'll need to negotiate. And as you mentioned, I'm an expert negotiator." He leaned in, his voice barely above a whisper, yet filled with dark demand. "You put yourself in my path. You possess something I want. Why act surprised when I take what you so foolishly dangle in front of me, even if it means you get more than you bargained for?"

"That wasn't my intent," she protested. A hint of panic edged her words. "You know it wasn't."

"But it is the result. Now we're going somewhere private, somewhere we won't be overheard or interrupted, and we're going to figure out precisely what it will take to seal this devil's bargain. Because nothing—not our engagement, not consummation of our engagement and definitely not my late wife's infamous cousin—will stand in the way of my getting that necklace. Are we clear?"

Kat's uneven breathing shattered the sudden silence between them and her creamy complexion grew stark. She stared at him, her brilliant eyes dark with frustration. He expected her to cave. She didn't. Somehow she found the presence to gather her self-control and confront him with a look of total defiance. "No man tells me what to do. Not even my future fiancé."

In that moment Gabe realized he would do whatever it took to have this woman, regardless of who and what he knew her to be. How was that possible? His late wife had gone into explicit detail about her notorious cousin. He'd witnessed Kat's fall from grace with his own eyes. She was precisely the sort of woman he avoided at all costs. He attempted to put his attraction down to the superficial resemblance between the cousins—both fine-boned and sable-haired. But Jessa had possessed eyes as black as ink, her hair equally so, lacking that hint of fire buried deep within the dark strands. And her features were cheerleader pretty versus elegantly stunning. She'd also lacked the womanly curves that gave Kat's Dior suit such eye-catching definition. In addition, his late wife's sweet, compliant personality couldn't have been any more dissimilar from her cousin's prickly defiance. Not that who—or what—this woman was made the least difference. Only one thing mattered to him and nothing would come between him and his Heart's Desire.

"If you want to squirm your way back into Matilda's good graces as much as I want my family's necklace, you'll do whatever is required. And if that means a legally consummated agreement, than that's what you'll do." She started to protest and he cut her off without compunction. "Anything you have to say can be said in a more private setting than this."

"But—"

"Not. *Here*."

She folded her arms across her chest. "Well, I'm not going to your place. So, it looks like it'll have to be your office, or nowhere."

"Fine. If you want to do it in my office, my office it is. Just let me lock the door and we can get this over with. Which do you prefer, desk or couch?"

She backed up a telling step. "Neither."

"Then I suggest we go somewhere private in order to discuss the situation. And that would be my place. It has the added advantage of giving the impression that my future wife has just flown in from overseas and we can't wait to be alone to…consummate our engagement."

"Which I have no intention of doing," she shot back.

He gestured toward the door. "Shall we?" She hesitated and he fought for patience. "By all means stand up for yourself. But I suggest you choose your battles. Fighting over every single issue is going to be exhausting, and frankly, it's pointless. If we can't agree on something as simple as where to hold our discussion, we might as well put an end to this farce right now."

"Fine. We'll go to your place. But all we'll be doing is talking."

"An excellent place to start."

He didn't give her time to come up with any further arguments. He ushered her from the office, then from the building, and into his car for the drive to Medina. They accomplished the vast portion of the trip in taut silence, whatever slumbered between them seething just beneath the surface, slowly intensifying until it reached almost unbearable levels.

They pulled into the drive of the sprawling estate fronting Lake Washington and Kat spared him a swift, startled glance. "It's beautiful," she murmured. Could she sound any more surprised?

"Wait until you see the views of the lake."

He led the way to the front door, entered his code and, without giving Kat warning, swept her into his arms and carried her over the threshold. The instant he set her on her feet, she attempted to pull away, but he didn't give her the chance.

"Welcome to my home, Ms. Malloy."

He could never explain what happened next, what sort of insanity seized him. He heard the voice in his head again, the dark, insidious voice that echoed with unmistakable demand. *Take the woman! She's the one.* Maybe he caved to temptation because he'd wanted her from the instant she'd walked into his office on those sexy peep-toed Valentino pumps with their "screw the world" siren-red spike heels. Or maybe he did it because she so clearly didn't want him. Or maybe it was to make a statement about who would be in charge of this unholy union. Whatever the reason, he took her hand in his to yank her into his arms. At the same instant, he lowered his head and took her mouth in a kiss of sheer demand.

The moment their hands and lips touched, passion exploded, a spark that flared to life, followed by a burn of need that flashed between them, melded them, connected them in a way he'd never experienced before. It flashed from mouth to fingertip before centering in his palm and sinking inward, straight through to his bones where it became part of the very fabric of his being. Desire crashed down on him, so insistent and undeniable that it took every ounce of the ice-cold discipline he was renowned for to keep himself under some semblance of control. To stop himself from carrying her off to his bedroom and consummating her proposal in every conceivable way.

And in that moment Gabe discovered that he couldn't maintain his self-control. Didn't want to. He deepened the kiss and allowed the insanity to consume him. More than anything he was driven to put his mark on her, brand her with his possession. To claim her for his own.

His woman. His future fiancée. His mate.

The one.

Two

Kat had no idea what Gabe Moretti had done to her.

A kiss. Just a simple kiss. That's all it should have been.

But the instant his lips touched hers, desire crashed down on her, a desire unlike anything she'd ever experienced before. One minute she'd been her own person, and the next she'd become someone else, someone who burned. Who needed. Who wanted with every fiber of her being.

No man had ever touched her like this. Not physically. Not emotionally. She'd worked so hard to protect herself, to build barriers that resisted all attempts to get too close. And yet, with one kiss this man—her soon-to-be fiancé— had swept away those barriers as though they were no more than flimsy tissue paper. How was it possible?

Even more distressing was the kiss itself, a kiss that actually sparked and burned, as though she'd touched a live wire. A kiss that had her sinking into him, opening to him, giving herself without thought or hesitation. If he chose to strip her naked right there in the foyer, she wouldn't have lifted a finger to stop him. Wouldn't? *Couldn't*. She could no more control her reaction to him than she could control the ebb and flow of the tide or the rising and setting of the sun.

He deepened the kiss and she yielded to him, allowed the insanity to consume her. She wanted him to put his mark on her, brand her with his possession. Claim her for his own.

He was her man. Her future fiancé. Her mate.

The one.

The instant the thought settled, she fought it. With a sharp cry, she wriggled free of Gabe's arms, even though it felt as though she were ripping away part of herself. She took a stumbling step backward. Then another and another until she felt the solid wood of his front door pressing against her spine.

No. Oh, no, no, no. How could she start over, wipe the slate clean, if she gave herself to this man? He belonged to an unwelcome past, along with Jessa and the scandal. Kat's plan from the start was to cut those ties and knot each and every dangling thread. Becoming engaged to Gabe had been part of that plan, but a temporary part, discarded as quickly as possible with no emotional involvement. Instead, those ties wrapped around her, tightening until she strangled beneath their pull and drag. Somehow, she'd lost who she was and who she'd meant to become, trapped within a web of Gabe's making, one of dark desire and need.

"What did you just do to me?" she demanded in a low voice.

"I kissed you."

She shook her head and felt the knot at the nape of her neck give, the heaviness of her hair loosening to tumble down her back. For some reason it signaled a final betrayal, a surrender she neither wanted, nor could avoid. A loss of the worst sort…of herself. Their kiss couldn't have lasted longer than a moment or two and yet look at what he'd done to her. Or rather, look at how he'd caused her to come undone. She'd always taken such pride in her cool poise, knowing that others might want, but could never take, not while she held herself at a careful distance. But with one touch, Gabe had stripped all that away.

"That was no kiss." She lifted trembling fingers to her mouth, where palm and lips both throbbed in tempo. "It burned. How did you do that?"

Something flickered in his golden gaze, almost as though he'd made an unexpected connection. "It just happened. I don't know how or why."

"Did it…" She moistened her lips. They felt warm and swollen…and delightfully sensitive. "Did it happen with Jessa? Is this a Moretti thing?"

A sooty eyebrow shot upward. "A Moretti thing?" he repeated, amusement lacing the question. He shook his head. "No, I suspect if it's anything, it's a Dante thing."

"Dante?" Did he mean the same Dantes who'd created his mother's necklace? The Dantes she one day hoped to work for? That didn't make any sense. "I don't understand."

"I don't either, but I will." He took a step in her direction and she tensed. To her relief, he didn't come any closer. "I don't know about you, but I need a drink. And I don't mean ice water."

"It's barely noon," she protested.

"I need a drink," he repeated. He gestured toward a room that opened off the foyer. "If you'll wait for me in the study, I'll arrange for lunch."

"I'd like to freshen up." She glanced around, an unwelcome helplessness settling over her. "Where…?"

"There's a bathroom off the study."

Praying that her shaky three-inch heels would hold her for the length of time it took to cross the wooden foyer floor, she headed in the direction he indicated and entered the study. It was a surprisingly charming room, beautifully appointed. As much as she'd have liked to linger and admire the heartwood floors and antique furniture, she continued on to the bathroom. One glance at the mirror confirmed her worst fears.

She didn't just look like a woman who'd been kissed senseless. She looked like a woman who'd been stripped bare. Exposed. Left utterly defenseless. That had happened only once before and she'd sworn she'd never allow it to happen again. And yet it had. Somehow Gabriel Moretti had found a way in and unlocked the Pandora's Box she kept buried in the deepest, darkest part of herself. And he'd done it with a single kiss. How was that possible?

And what was that bizarre heat that had flared between them? It hadn't been passion alone. Something more burned there. Something she didn't have a hope of controlling, that instead directed and ordained, as though fate had seized hold of her life and set it on a new and unalterable path. She didn't have a single doubt that path led straight into Gabe's arms, the one place she had no intention of going and the one place she most wanted to explore.

Lucky, lucky Jessa.

Kat lifted a hand to her mouth, stricken at how her fingers trembled. And her eyes… Dark, filled with pain. A window to her every thought and emotion. With her hair tumbling around her shoulders and her mouth ripe and swollen she appeared— Oh, God. *Ravished.* And with one kiss. What would happen when he took the embrace farther than a single kiss?

She shoved the thought away. This would never do. She simply wouldn't allow it. Opening her purse, she swiftly rebuilt the feminine barriers women through the ages had used to protect themselves. With her hair once again ruthlessly knotted at her nape and her makeup impeccably applied, she felt better. She'd feel a whole lot better if she could somehow shield the expression in her eyes.

She closed them and remembered. Remembered all she'd gone through, all she'd achieved to date. All she intended to accomplish in the future. She remembered the past, and the immense debt she owed her grandmother for taking her in after her parents' deaths. Of her struggle the past five years and how she'd ruthlessly pinched every penny of the inheritance she received from the trust account her parents set up. Life had been beyond difficult until her finances had taken a swift upward swing eighteen months ago, enough of a swing to indulge in a few excellent pieces of designer clothing and shoes.

But most important of all was her desperation to reconcile with the woman who'd been her entire world until five years ago. Not to mention her ultimate goal and eventual destination…San Francisco and the shot at a job as a jewelry designer for Dantes. It steadied her as nothing else could.

When she checked the mirror again, she saw a woman in charge of her own destiny. A woman who could resist Gabriel Moretti. She took a deep, calming breath, praying that's what Gabe saw, as well.

She returned to the study to discover him pouring drinks. He glanced at her and a knowing gleam shot through his distinctive gold eyes. "Feel better?" he asked.

"Much."

"Drink?"

She shrugged. Why not? "Thanks. Neat, please."

"I've arranged for lunch. It should be ready shortly. I also put a call in to my attorney. I'll have Tom Blythe pull together some sort of agreement. I can assure you he'll be discreet." Gabe approached and handed her a leaded crystal tumbler. Their fingertips brushed, intensifying the faint sizzle and burn that hummed between them. For some reason, it centered in her palm and in her lips. Odd. Very odd. And very distracting. "So, why don't you present your proposition and we'll discuss how we should go from there?"

His businesslike attitude helped steady her, earning her gratitude. "It's fairly simple. We make a point of a first meeting, somewhere public so it's both noticed and notable. We date for a set number of months. Announce our engagement. Allow the engagement to run its course until…" She took a quick drink, the burn of liquor helping to keep her composed and focused. She repeated the word, with more finality this time. "Until." She still couldn't bring herself to say the words, words that threatened to break her heart. *Until Gam died.*

"I think there's a little more involved than that," Gabe warned.

She lifted an eyebrow. "Such as?"

"The venue for our meeting. How long we should date. How and when to announce the engagement. How best to handle Matilda. At what point the transfer of property occurs." His voice dropped and his gaze heated. "Not to mention, the…consummation of our agreement."

This time he didn't even have to touch her for her to come undone. She took another quick drink before speaking, praying her voice didn't reveal any hint of her inner turmoil. Why him? Of all people, why Jessa's husband? "I suggest the most trendy, public venue possible for our initial dates. I'm a bit out of touch these days, so you would know better than I where that would be."

"Acceptable."

"As for announcing our engagement, I suggest we wait three to six months."

"One."

She shook her head. "No one is going to buy that."

"I believe they will." He smiled in a way that caused nerves to skitter along her spine and the tug of desire to intensify. "Especially when they see I can't keep my hands off you."

"Three," she bargained desperately. "Three months."

"One."

Her mouth tightened. "People won't believe it. And I need them to believe."

"People will believe I'm merely a fool in love," he stated matter-of-factly. "Unfortunately, your reputation precedes you, so I'm afraid they won't be quite so generous in their opinion of you. And when I end our engagement and cut off all contact with you, I suspect your flirtation with respectability will also end."

Kat got it then. Every ounce of color drained from her face and the breath stuttered in her lungs. "When you end the engagement, you hope to confirm the general consensus, don't you?" The question escaped in a thready whisper. "Why? Why would you do that?"

His tarnished eyes burned like the fires from hell. "Let's call it an engagement gift from Jessa. Of course, you can refuse, take the moral high ground and walk away from the deal. But something tells me you won't, even if it means finding yourself in the middle of another scandal with your reputation, once again, ripped to shreds."

"If you destroy my reputation, how am I supposed to convince my grandmother I've changed?"

"I don't plan to destroy your reputation while Matilda is still alive. In the meantime, she'll believe whatever I tell her. If I put my stamp of approval on you, she'll go along with it, mainly because she wants to believe. But we'll know the truth, won't we, Kat? And eventually, so will the rest of Seattle."

Pain tore through her. *Leave,* a small voice insisted. *Go now. Nothing is worth this.* Maybe she would have if it hadn't been for one unfortunate detail. Something happened when he'd kissed her. Something that changed everything. She couldn't explain it. Didn't understand how or why it altered the playing field. She simply knew it did.

Somehow, some way, he'd forged a connection between them, one she couldn't escape. Didn't want to escape. Oh, she knew it wouldn't last. Of course it wouldn't. But it compelled her to stay until that connection broke, or dissipated, or ran its course, no matter how painful that course might be.

She'd come to Seattle with one purpose in mind—a reconciliation with Gam. Nothing else mattered beyond that, especially now that their time together was so terribly finite. Or so Kat thought until her meeting with Gabe Moretti, until she'd walked into his office and been knocked sideways by a desire so paramount, nothing else seemed to matter. She closed her eyes. Okay, fine. So, she'd just proven to herself that she had base desires like every other woman in the world. That didn't change her goals, not really. Once that desire ran its course and once she'd made Gam's final days as happy as possible, she'd be free to move on and start over with a clean slate. The thought hovered before her like a golden dream. A dream she'd spent the past five years believing impossible to achieve.

"Well?" he demanded "Do you agree to my proposition?"

She struggled to conceal how much the small growl rippling through his question unsettled her. "Let's say I'm open to further negotiation."

If he felt any triumph at the concession, he didn't show it. If anything, his tension grew. "I insist on a legally binding agreement that you'll give me Heart's Desire."

"One that goes both ways," she shot right back. "I need you to promise to stay engaged to me and treat me appropriately while my grandmother's alive. Trust me when I say I intend to spell out in explicit detail just what 'appropriately' entails."

"Fair enough."

"Then we're agreed?"

He shook his head. "I expect you to consummate our agreement."

Heat stormed across her cheekbones. She turned on her heel and paced the room, pausing to examine a small free-flowing statuette, the dark polished wood exquisitely carved. She ran a finger along the smooth lines, wishing just once her life could run along equally smooth lines. A fruitless wish since it never had.

Even as a child her life had been one of turmoil, her grandmother the only steady, unwavering influence in her life. From the tender age of five, when her parents had died from a virus while on a humanitarian mission, her grandmother had been her world. Her rock.

Until Jessa changed all that.

She turned from the statuette and faced Gabe. "I suspect 'consummate our agreement' is your not-so-subtle way of telling me that you want to sleep with me."

"Not at all."

Confusion swept through her. Had she misunderstood? "Oh. Then what do you mean?"

He silently approached. "Sleeping won't be involved in our consummation. Sex will."

She didn't dare agree to that. It offered the possibility for far too many pitfalls. She assumed he wanted the necklace as badly as she wanted to reconcile with her grandmother. That didn't mean she'd risk everything on that one assumption. She forced herself to throw a quick, amused glance over her shoulder. "Sorry. That won't happen."

"You think not?"

She turned to face him. "Let's just say I'm saving myself for marriage," she said, perfectly serious. Not that he believed her.

Laughter escaped, the sound dark and rich and sliding through her veins like the sweetest of wines. "I like your sense of humor."

She fought to keep her barriers strong, to ignore the sensations lapping at her in ever increasing waves. "I didn't realize I'd said anything funny."

His eyes darkened, the color a tawny antique gold. They held her, warmed and warned her, made promises that filled her with longing and dread. "Fine," he said at last. "If you insist on waiting until you're married, I'll accept that."

But she knew he didn't mean the words, that he thought she'd cave to her baser instincts. Sadly, it was a strong possibility. "Then we have a deal?" she asked.

"We do." He tipped his glass toward hers. The crystal touched, releasing a soft, sweet note, the purity of it at odds with their unwholesome agreement.

He waited until they'd both taken a drink before setting the two tumblers aside. Then he reached for her, tugging her into his arms. Alarm shot through her. "What are you doing?"

"Consummating our agreement."

She struggled to free herself without success. "But, that's not what you said."

"I agreed to wait if you insisted we do so. That didn't mean I couldn't tempt you to change your mind." He lowered his head until his mouth hovered just above hers. "Are you tempted, Kat?"

He'd thought this kiss would be different.

It wasn't.

If anything, the bond created between them the first time they kissed intensified. Heat flared and splashed, rushing through his veins, sinking into his bones, and spiking his desire to an unbearable level. With a soft moan, her lips parted beneath his, allowing him to slip within and savor the honeyed warmth. Never had he tasted anything so delicious. It was as though her flavor had been specifically designed for him, designed to please and arouse, to tempt and satisfy. He couldn't seem to get enough. He wanted more.

He found the buttons to her suit jacket and released them. The edges parted a tantalizing few inches and beneath he found a scrap of black lace that revealed almost as much as it concealed. Her skin was a lovely shade of cream, so soft and pale against the darkness of her bra. The tops of her breasts rose above the fragile cups and her breath quickened beneath his gaze. Gently, tenderly, he shaped her breasts in his hands, recalling how they'd appeared when he'd found her in Winters' bed.

Stunning. Utterly stunning.

Her nipples tightened within his palms, pressing against the fragile lace in response to his caress and signaling her arousal. Fair enough. He was equally aroused, tight and heavy with the need to make this woman his own. He guided her backward toward the sofa, the imperative to take her and make her his beyond anything he'd experienced before. She bumped into the couch and with a startled cry, fell backward. She lay there against a deep green background, her jacket open, her hair once again free of its tight knot and tumbling like black fire around her pale shoulders. She stared up at him, her eyes picking up the color of the fabric and echoing its forest-shadowed hue.

He expected to see the knowing look of a woman who'd found herself in this position innumerous times in her checkered past. Instead, an innate feminine defenselessness gleamed there, a bewilderment he couldn't quite accept. Even so, he didn't sense any deception on her part, though he'd be a fool to believe anything this woman said or did. She played people, he reminded himself. She lied more easily than she told the truth. She was a woman who'd mastered the art of deception and manipulation, no doubt while still in the cradle.

And yet, still he wanted her.

He followed her down, planting his arms on either side of her head. His hands sank into her hair. The thick strands flowed through his fingers like silk, the slumberous fire within a fitting match for the fire that burned in her pale green gaze.

"Why do you wear it tied up in knots?" he asked.

"To keep it under control."

He offered an understanding smile. "You like control." It wasn't a question.

"Of myself," she conceded. She shifted against the cushions, a wry smile flickering across her mouth. "Not that I seem to possess any. At least, not with you."

"Seems we're in the same boat." He hadn't meant to concede so much. But this woman stripped him of control. Control and barriers and the ability to think straight. His reaction to her was as visceral as it was overwhelming. "But there's an easy solution."

"If you mean making love, I don't consider that an easy solution."

He couldn't prevent a cynical laugh. "Making love?"

Her lashes drifted downward and she shrugged. "Having sex?" she suggested dispassionately.

"Closer. And trust me…" He feathered a kiss across her jawline. She shuddered in reaction and he smiled, nipping at the soft, tender skin. "It's the simplest solution there is when you consider all the problems between us."

She stiffened ever so slightly. "This just adds another layer of complication."

He skated lower, along the long line of her neck. He could

feel her pulse against his mouth, practically taste her pounding need. "A delicious complication." Her breath escaped in soft little gasps, the sound fueling his arousal, the imperative to make her his building toward an overpowering desperation. If he didn't have her soon he just might go insane. "Not to mention a necessary one." Very, very necessary.

"Why is it necessary?" she asked.

Was she joking? His mouth settled in the satiny crook between neck and shoulder and he planted a series of kisses there. "We need to give the impression that we're crazy about each other. That we can't keep our hands to ourselves. That all we want is to get through whatever social function we're attending so we can escape to the nearest dark corner in order to get naked as fast as humanly possible."

She squeezed her eyes closed. "That doesn't mean we have to actually do it."

He swept her suit jacket off her shoulders and halfway down her arms. "I don't want there to be any question about the fact that we're lovers. Not a single doubt. It's the only way to explain the swiftness of our engagement. Women have a knack for sensing these things. They'll know if we're faking it."

"We're not faking our attraction. Maybe that's enough."

He levered upward. "You've been intimate with a man. You know damn well that changes things."

Her eyes opened and she gazed at him with an odd defiance. "Do I?"

"Oh, please. Don't try to play the innocent with me."

"I guess that would be pointless, wouldn't it?"

"Considering I was the one who found you with Winters? Yes." He didn't want to go there, didn't want to allow the shadow of another man to ruin the moment or slip between them. Not now. Not when he finally had her where he wanted her. "Be reasonable, Kat. You've had lovers. Think about how it is with them. The way you speak to him. Those small caresses and looks that only lovers exchange. The knowledge you gain when you've shared a bed. When you've been stripped bare and possessed by a man. It comes through in everything you do and say. In how you react on both a conscious and subconscious level."

"And we need to build that level of familiarity?"

How could she doubt it? "Yes. I want to touch you and have everyone watching sense that I've touched you just that way in bed. I want the same expression on your face and in your eyes, so everyone in the vicinity can tell that the last time you looked at me that way, our bodies were mated in the most intimate way possible."

She shuddered again and he knew his words had seduced her almost as much as his touch. "I don't want to do this." But somehow he suspected her words were meant for herself, rather than for his benefit.

His drew his fingertip along the edge of her bra, and a soft flush colored the tops of her breasts, while her breathing kicked up a notch. He lowered his head and caught her pebbled nipple between his teeth through the black lace, dampening it. The air burst from her lungs on a small cry that had him tightening in reaction, the urge to take her beyond anything he'd ever experienced before, the demand pure and elemental and unceasing. Hooking his fingers into the cups of the bra, he dragged them downward, exposing her.

She was every bit as lovely as he remembered, maybe more so. Full and round, her breasts were tipped by nipples the same shade as the skin of a ripe peach. More than anything he wanted to taste them, to see if they were as succulent as the fruit they resembled. He suspected they were. Before he could put thought to action, a brisk knock sounded at the door.

"Mr. Moretti? Lunch is ready."

Kat froze, passion transitioning to utter horror. She stared at him in disbelief. "What are we doing?"

"I believe it's called foreplay," he offered helpfully. He glanced down at her breasts. "Possibly an appetizer."

"Not any longer, it isn't." She dragged her bra into position before shoving at his shoulders. "Please, get off me."

"No appetizer?" She simply stared at him and he sighed. "I gather that means dessert's out of the question, too."

"I don't eat dessert."

He grinned. "I'd be happy to have yours."

"We're not talking about food, are we?"

Gabe spared a final glance at her breasts. "I guess it depends on your point of view." He stood and held out his hand. To his surprise, she accepted his assistance. "I assume you want to freshen up again."

She released a sigh. "Is there any point?"

"Not really." He ran his fingers through her hair, combing out the tangles while she tackled the buttons of her jacket, then attempted to smooth out a few of the creases without much success. "Besides, I like your hair down. It makes you appear more human."

A swift smile flashed across her mouth—a mouth naked of any artifice and still swollen from his kisses, he noted with satisfaction. "Human? Versus what?"

"Something unreal. Remote. Untouchable and untouched." He gave the hem of her suit jacket a gentle tug, amused to realize that the buttons weren't in the right holes. He should mention it. He really should. Or maybe not since it added immeasurably to that "human" quality. "And we both know that's not the real you."

Her expression closed down. "Since you know so much about me."

"I know enough." He gestured toward the door to the study. "Shall we?"

"I'd really prefer returning to my hotel. I'm still rather jetlagged."

He draped an arm around her waist and urged her forward. "Food will help. Dennis is an excellent chef. I'm sure you'll appreciate a good meal before I drive you to your hotel."

She didn't protest any further, following him into the informal dining room, a small, intimate area that overlooked the sprawl of green grass that tumbled toward the lake. She paused by the windows and seemed to relax infinitesimally.

"Like it?" Gabe asked.

"Who wouldn't?"

Jessa, he almost said, before catching himself in the nick of time. "Some prefer city life."

She lifted a shoulder in a quick shrug. "It has its advantages. Personally, I get tired of all the noise and constant press of humanity."

"Which is why I bought this place last year. That and the view."

She glanced at him over her shoulder. "You've owned it for only a year?"

"We lived in an apartment near my office," he answered the unspoken question. He gestured toward the table. "Shall we?"

She took her seat without another word, avoiding his gaze. Maybe it was because he'd mentioned Jessa, the ghost of his late wife creating an uncomfortable silence. He should despise Kat for the hell she'd put her cousin through, for her overall disdain toward right or wrong. For taking whatever she wanted, regardless of who she hurt in the process. At least in his mother's case, she'd attempted to do the right thing by leaving Dominic when he married another.

That didn't change the fact than when he held Kat in his arms, nothing mattered except making her his own.

Need—a need far greater than any he'd experienced with Jessa—stripped away every other impulse. There had to be an explanation. There had to be a reason he'd allow this woman to demolish lines he'd made an unwavering commitment to keep inviolate.

And he had no doubt where to place the blame. His father had been a Dante. Immoral. A cheat. A liar. Gabe had fought the Dante genes with the first breath he'd taken, and would no doubt continue to fight them until he gasped out his last. From the time he'd first understood the devastation his father had wrought in his mother's life, he'd made up his mind that he'd never become his father. Never turn into the man who'd caused his family so much suffering.

And yet… Somehow, some way those Dante genes were responsible for what had happened when he'd first touched Kat. There couldn't be any other explanation. Oh, he'd heard the ridiculous stories from his mother, though he'd never believed them. But now he wondered if there weren't some small grain of truth to what she'd revealed. Because judging by his reaction to Kat, the inner awareness coupled with the electric spark when they'd first touched, he'd been hit by the infamous Dantes' Inferno. He'd heard it described as a sort of itching burn experienced when future lovers first touched—or so his mother had claimed. As far as Gabe was concerned it was nothing more than a fairy tale his father had used to get his mother into bed.

He released his breath in a frustrated sigh. He'd hoped never to have to approach his father's family. Despised them, one and all, for their part in his mother's heartbreak and sorrow. But this Inferno business was too bizarre not to pursue. Tomorrow he'd get details, lots and lots of details, before cutting himself off from the Dantes once more. And then he'd figure out what to do about this Inferno nonsense, and more importantly, how to eradicate it.

Dennis entered with their salads before making himself scarce. Kat picked at her food for a few minutes before returning her fork to her plate. "This is ridiculous," she stated. Her gaze flashed to Gabe's. "Why am I here? I mean, seriously. What's left to discuss? You've wrung just about every possible concession from me. Can't you just let it go at that?"

He sipped the Chablis accompanying their lunch while he considered his response. "If we can't share a simple meal that doesn't bode well for our engagement."

Her mouth tilted upward in a dry smile and his gaze settled there, that blasted inner voice urging him to take those lush lips in an endless kiss and the hell with everything else, including food or consequence. "What doesn't bode well for our engagement is that you despise me."

He forced himself to look away from her mouth and focus instead on his salad. "You'll have to find a way to live with it, I'm afraid."

"Or you could cut me some slack."

He couldn't help laughing. So she wanted to be let off the hook already, did she? "Not a chance in hell, sweetheart."

She regarded him in silence for a few moments. "We're not engaged yet, which means that I still have choices available to me—including leaving."

He shrugged, unimpressed by the threat. "You can try, but we both know that you want your grandmother's inheritance too much to walk away."

"I want to reconcile with my grandmother," she corrected. "I want it very much. But not enough to spend endless months with someone who plans to make our time together so painful. Nothing's worth that."

Gabe lifted an eyebrow. "I gather we're negotiating again?"

"Yes."

Interesting. "What offer are you putting on the table?"

"I'd like to start over. Clean slate."

He shook his head. "That's not possible. You can't change what happened. What you did."

She hesitated before responding. "But we can choose to put it behind us and move on. I won't spend endless months with you, endure an engagement and…and pretend in public to be something we're not, all the while being punished by you over past events. I can't handle that."

"And if I don't agree?"

She tossed her napkin to the table. "Then you'll have to decide how badly you want your mother's necklace." She stood. "Apologize to Dennis if you would, please. I'm sure he'll understand if you explain that jetlag has finally caught up with me—which it has."

"I'll drive you back to Seattle." He could see her budding refusal and cut her off before she could say anything more. "I'll drive you back," he repeated.

She nodded, though he suspected it was more a result of exhaustion than because she saw the sense in accepting his offer. "I'll be at my hotel all day tomorrow. Feel free to call and give me your decision."

"Clean slate and a polite engagement?"

"Or I return to Europe and neither of us gets what we want."

"We don't need to wait until tomorrow. I accept your offer."

She didn't show the slightest relief. She simply nodded again and started toward the front door. He stopped her there. Unable to explain why he did it, he rebuttoned her suit jacket so the buttons and holes were properly aligned, then dropped a gentle kiss on her forehead. Hell, next he'd be tucking her into bed. Alone, no less. His mouth tightened.

He didn't have a clue what was going on, but first thing in the morning he intended to find out.

And then he intended to fix it so he could get his life back to normal.

Three

Early the next morning, Gabe left Kat a voicemail to warn he'd be out of touch that day. He took his private jet from Seattle to San Francisco, the flight proving uneventful. A car awaited him at his destination and he used the transit time into the city to finalize details on the Atkinson project. Several times he caught himself rubbing his palm, a burning itch centered there, one which had appeared the moment he first touched Kat, and continued to throb ever since. It was downright bizarre.

Since it was Saturday, they didn't experience much traffic and, in record time, pulled in front of the head office for Dantes, the jewelry empire that specialized in the one-of-a-kind Dante fire diamonds. As hoped, the place was deserted, nary a Dante in sight. Bad enough that he needed to speak to the family patriarch—his grandfather, Primo—without running into any of the legitimate side of the family. Most of them didn't even know he existed, which was precisely how Gabe preferred to keep it. He signed in at the front reception desk, accepted the guest pass and crossed to the bank of elevators that led to the executive offices. He exited on one of the upper echelon floors of the high-rise building and stepped into a foyer where even the air exuded luxury and opulence.

From the end of a long, shadow-draped corridor, a woman approached, no doubt to escort him to the office Primo still maintained, though Gabe's research indicated that his father's first legitimate son, Sev, ran Dantes. The patriarch and founder of the firm semi-retired not long after Gabe's father, Dominic, had died in a sailing accident which also claimed his wife, Laura, orphaning Sev and his three brothers. Primo's health had taken a serious hit due to the death of his eldest son, forcing him to hand the reins over to Sev. Of course, the Dantes pretended not to know about the existence of Gabe's mother, the twins, or that Dominic planned to marry her after divorcing his wife. Not that Gabe believed his father actually would have. Like all Dantes, his father liked to have his cake and eat it, too. Why else would he have been sailing with his wife?

He returned his attention to the woman and froze, instantly recognizing her hair, a distinctive blend of varying shades of brown. "What the bloody hell are you doing here?" he demanded.

She shot a quick, nervous glance over her shoulder. "Hush. I don't want anyone to hear you."

"You haven't answered my question, Lucia." Every protective instinct he possessed flared into life. He snatched her into his arms and gave her a swift, hard hug, one she returned with equal ferocity. "What are you doing here?" he repeated.

She stepped free of the embrace and offered an impish

grin, though he sensed a deeper emotion seething beneath her cheerful exterior. "I work for Primo."

"Damn it to hell." Gabe shot his hands through his hair. "Does he know who you are?"

A hint of familiar fire sparked to life in her eyes. "Of course not. I wouldn't do that without warning you first."

"*Why?*" he asked roughly. "Why, by all that's holy, would you want to have anything to do with the Dantes, after what *he* did to Mom?"

"*He.* You mean Dad." That single word contained a world of heartbreak and cut Gabe to the core. Of the three of them, his twin, Lucia, had held out the longest, certain that someday Dominic Dante would ride in on his white horse and sweep them off to live in his castle. Even after his death, she'd thought the Dantes would claim them as their own. Needless to say, that had never happened. Eventually, the fairy tale shattered, leaving nothing but devastation in its wake. "You can use the word, Gabriel. *Dad.* I swear it won't set your tongue on fire."

"Don't be so sure," he retorted. "And he wasn't our father. He was *their* father."

An all too familiar expression swept across her elegant features, one that would have done the most stubborn mule proud. "He was ours, too. Just because you don't want to know our family doesn't mean I don't."

His head jerked back as though she'd slapped him. "They are *not* our family."

"You may not want them for family, but that doesn't change the fact that they—"

Lucia broke off and for a split second her chin quivered, while tears burned in her distinctive blue-green eyes. Their mother's eyes. That, more than anything else, nearly sent Gabe to his knees. His sister, his strong, resilient twin, the woman who faced every adversity with a brave smile, hovered on the verge of tears. Without a word, he gathered her close and simply held her.

"Does it really mean that much to you?" he murmured.

"Yes." Her voice held a firm, if muffled, note. "They're all the family we have left."

He flinched. "We have each other. We'll always have each other."

"There's never been any question of that." She pulled back and cupped his face, her gaze brimming with adoration. "You're my big brother, even if it's only by four minutes."

"Five."

She laughed through her tears. "Okay, five. You've always been there when I needed you most. If you hadn't come to my rescue when—"

"Don't." It had been a brutal time, even worse than learning of their father's death. He smoothed back a lock of his sister's hair, the color so different from his own, a glorious mix of browns, from the very palest shade to the deepest. In appearance, they couldn't be any more different. But at heart... "There's no point going there."

She nodded her agreement. "You're right." Pulling free of his arms, she frowned. To his relief, she'd conquered her tears and appeared almost normal again. Almost. "So what are you doing here? I mean, since Primo isn't family."

Gabe spared a swift glance down the deserted hallway. "I have a question to ask him, one only he can answer."

She tilted her head to one side, avid curiosity sparkling in her gaze. "What question?"

"A none of your business question."

Her eyes narrowed, sharpened, and she took a step closer, catching his hand in hers. It had always been that way between them. Maybe it was because they were twins. Or maybe because they'd grown up fatherless. But there'd always been a deep, emotional connection between them. "Something's happened. What is it?"

"Nothing that concerns you, brat." He gestured in the direction she'd come. "I'd like to get this meeting over with, if you don't mind."

She lifted her shoulders in a quick shrug. "Fine. Be all brooding and mysterious. You know you'll tell me eventually." She tossed him a teasing grin. "Admit it. You've never been able to resist me."

He wrapped her up in a quick embrace and dropped a swift, affectionate kiss on her brow. "True enough." He shot another glance toward Primo's office. "Before I meet with him, tell me what to expect. What's he like?"

She started to respond, then hesitated, shaking her head. "No, I don't believe I will. I think you should figure that out for yourself."

Aw, hell. That wasn't the least like her. She'd always been the most unguarded of all of them, her heart open to anyone and everyone—which had led her to fall in love with a bastard who'd ripped her to shreds. After that she'd grown more cautious, but never with Gabe. Her secrets were his. Until now, apparently.

"What's wrong, Lucia? What are you hiding?"

To his concern, distress peeked through, warning she hadn't fully regained her equilibrium. "I'm not hiding anything, other than my identity. I wanted to meet my grandfather in order to see what he's like without his knowing that I'm Cara Moretti's daughter. So, I'm using my married name."

"As far as I know they're only aware of my existence," he attempted to reassure. "I don't think they've discovered I have a twin."

"No, they haven't," she confirmed.

"He's hurt you somehow." He cut her off before she could speak. "Don't deny it. I can tell when you're in pain."

Lucia started to protest, but must have realized the sheer futility of it. He simply knew her too well. She released her breath in a sigh. "Okay, fine. But, just so you know, it isn't due to anything Primo's done."

"Then, what is it?"

She turned on her heel and headed down the corridor, pausing outside the door leading to Primo's suite. She kept her back to him, her spine a rigid line. "I'm his employee," she confessed in a low voice. "He's very kind to employees."

"But?"

She glanced at him over her shoulder. This time she managed to control the tears, to keep her expression calm and pleasant, which only made it all the more tragic. "That's not who I am. It's not what I am." She took a moment to gather herself, before confessing, "Oh, Gabe, I don't want to work for him. I want to be his granddaughter. I want what we never had. Family." Before he had a chance to respond, she shoved open the door and swept inside. Crossing the outer office to a second door, she knocked briskly before opening it. "Mr. Moretti is here to see you."

"Send him in."

The voice was deep and rich, flavored with his Tuscan origins. It contained an irresistible lyricism, a haunting song that felt almost familiar, striking a visceral chord within Gabe, tugging at him. Drawing him in where he most resisted going. He hesitated, torn between comforting his sister and meeting his grandfather.

Lucia took the decision from him. She stepped back and shook her head. "I'm okay." Then she held out her fist, her index finger extended to form a small hook. He did the same, linking their fingers the way their mother had taught them from the time they were babies. It was a game the three of them played, a show of unity. A way to say "I love you." A wordless code to offer strength and support. "Go," she whispered, breaking contact.

If he lingered, he'd blow her cover, and he couldn't do that to her. "This isn't over," he warned in an undertone. Then he stepped into the room and came face-to-face with a man who revealed what Gabe would look like in another fifty or so years.

Primo slowly stood, drinking him in. "You look so much like your brother Severo, you could be twins," he marveled.

Gabe fought not to flinch. "I don't consider him my brother."

Primo shrugged. "This does not surprise me. It is understandable you would feel this way about all of us. What your father did was wrong."

Okay, that surprised him. "I agree."

His grandfather released a husky laugh. "You did not expect me to say that about my own son, eh?" He flipped open an intricately carved humidor resting on his desk and selected a cigar. He gestured toward the box. "Would you like?"

"I believe it's illegal to smoke those in an office."

Primo snorted. "What? You are going to call the cigar police on me?"

"That depends on how our conversation goes."

The two men stared at each other for a split second. Then Primo broke the silence with a loud laugh. He circled the desk and approached Gabe. Sweeping his grandson into his arms, he gave him a long, hard hug, slapping his back with an iron hand. "I never thought to see this day, Gabriel." He gave the name its Italian pronunciation.

Gabe stiffened, totally unprepared for both the embrace and how to handle it. Finally, he gave the old man a thump on the back. Based on Primo's gusty sigh, it seemed to satisfy him. He released Gabe and stepped back.

"I don't think you understand why I'm here," Gabe began.

Golden eyes, identical to his, stared at him. They were wise, ancient eyes, filled with understanding and sadness, joy and resignation. "I thank you for contacting me, even if it was not in order to meet your *nonno*."

Gabe lowered his head. "Aw, hell." This was definitely not going the way he'd intended.

"This is not going the way you intended, no?"

Crap. The Dante patriarch could even read his mind. Gabe looked up, deciding to be direct. After all, for better or worse, that's who he was. "No, it's not."

"You think…I come, I force myself to be polite to the old man. I ask my question. And I leave before he can touch my heart or infect my mind." Primo's index finger thumped first against Gabe's chest, then his temple. "But it is too late. There I am, like a…a—" He broke off with a frown. "What animal burrows in where it does not belong?"

"You, apparently."

Primo barked out another laugh. In a practiced move, he trimmed his cigar and lit it. "We keep the cigar a secret between the two of us, yes? Nonna will nag me into little pieces if she finds out. Then she will report me to my *dottore*."

How had it happened? How had this canny old man managed to get to him? Because he was right. Gabe had planned to show up, hold himself at a careful distance, ask his damn question and then get the hell out. Instead, he stood there, fascinated. Is that how it had been with his mother? Had Dominic been equally charming, burrowing through his mother's defenses until she'd given her heart and soul to the man who'd fathered her two children?

"I'm not like him." He had no idea where the words came

from. They were out before he even realized he intended to speak them.

A deep sadness flickered across Primo's expressive face. "No, you are not," he agreed softly. "Any more than Severo or Marco, Lazzaro or Nicolò are like him. You all possess a moral compass he lacked. I am sorry for what he did to you. And I am sorry I did not find you sooner."

Find him sooner? Was it possible the rest of the Dantes *didn't* know about him and Lucia? No. Not a chance. Not that he'd confront Primo over the issue. There wasn't any point. "It doesn't matter. I had no interest in knowing any of you."

Primo brushed aside the comment, refusing to accept it. "You are here now, are you not?"

Gabe caught himself rubbing the itch centered in his palm again, a gesture that drew his grandfather's attention and prompted an odd smile. "I'm only here because I have a question."

Primo settled a hip on the edge of his desk and blew out a stream of smoke, eyeing his grandson through the haze. The Cheshire Cat, all grin and knowing eyes. "Many questions, I would think."

"Just one."

"Fine." Primo gestured with his cigar. "You ask your question. I will answer if I am able."

"Something happened recently." Now that the time had come, he realized he didn't quite know how to phrase what had happened without sounding crazy. "Something…odd."

Laughter deepened the lines in the old man's face, one that contained a peculiar understanding. "Did it? Interesting." He examined the glowing tip of his cigar. "This odd thing that happened recently, I do not suppose it occurred with a woman?"

Gabe froze. "Son of a bitch," he whispered. "You know, don't you?"

"Know what?"

Gabe spun on his heel and stalked the length of the room, struggling to contain his anger. How was it possible? For years he'd perfected his iceman reputation, right up until Kat had swept into his office and utterly decimated it. And now his grandfather… Between the two of them, he was lucky to retain any control at all. More than anything he wanted to walk out and never return. But he couldn't. Not until he uncovered the truth.

He turned to face Primo, surrendering to the pressing demand for answers. "Okay, what the hell was it? All I did was touch her and—"

"And you burned for her." His grandfather gestured with his cigar. "Your palm. It itches, an itch that will not go away."

"Yes! Yes, damn it." He yanked at his tie, the knot threatening to choke him. "That's precisely what happened. What was it?"

"The Inferno, of course. Did Dominic never tell your mother about it?"

Gabe hesitated. "He told her some sort of fairy tale about Dantes being able to tell their soul mates with one touch."

"There you are, then. Your question, it is answered." Primo lifted a snowy eyebrow. "Is there anything else?"

"What do you mean, *is there anything else?*" His temper blew, scorching through the last of his iciness. "The Inferno? Are you serious? That's not real. It's simply another fairy tale, one told to our mother and exaggerated in the scandal sheets after Marco's little media stunt. But it doesn't actually exist."

"I assure you, *nipote*, it does exist. The Inferno is no fairy tale. You ignore it at your own risk."

Gabe's eyes narrowed. "Explain that. What risk?"

"You touched a woman." Primo's voice softened, yet the lyricism intensified. It wove a web with words, the music of his Tuscan origins wrapping around Gabe and sinking into him until it became part and parcel of who and what he was at the very core. "You felt the fire of The Inferno. Felt this itch and burn that will not stop. That is because this woman, she is your soul mate. Now you must marry her or suffer the consequences as your father did when he refused to marry his Inferno mate."

"What consequences?" Gabe demanded.

Primo's grip tightened on his cigar. "I told my Dominic to marry your mother." His accent deepened with raw emotion and his hands danced through the air, their sweeping movements leaving graceful swirls of smoke in their wake. "I warn him, do not turn from this woman. But he thought he could have it all—your mother, an Inferno soul mate, and the wealth Laura could bring to their marriage."

Primo encouraged his parents to marry? No. No, his father had claimed Primo had prevented the marriage. Had forbidden it. "I don't believe you."

Primo shrugged. "You may believe what you will, *nipote*. It will not change what happened. You see this marriage of Dominic's, how poorly it worked out for him. It has always been so with The Inferno." He kept his unwavering focus on Gabe, his calm sincerity giving weight to his claim. "We are different, Gabriel. Dantes only love one woman for all of their lives. We must follow where it leads, take the woman it selects for us, or suffer the consequences. And there are always consequences if we turn from The Inferno. Your father, he discovered the truth of this."

Gabe froze. That's when it hit him. Kat Malloy. If Primo was right, *she* was his Inferno mate. No. Oh, hell no. "I am *not* a Dante," he stated. Insisted. Or—*damn it*—did he beg? "This has nothing to do with me. It can't. I won't let it."

Sorrow tarnished Primo's eyes. "You have always been a Dante. You always will be a Dante."

"You're wrong." He rejected the premise with a cutting sweep of his hand. "I am nothing like Dominic. I refuse to be like him. Like any of you. I'm a Moretti."

"If you truly were, you would not experience The Inferno. But you have." Primo knocked ash off the end of his cigar and approached. He dropped a hand on Gabe's shoulder and gave it a hard squeeze. "I understand this resentment you feel for us. How you must despise us. But do not think for one moment that Dominic represents the Dantes. He is a Dante despite what he did to Cara and Laura and all his children. That is not how we raised him. The choices he made, they were his own, just as your choices are your own. You can choose to listen to what I have told you, or you can follow in the unfortunate footsteps of your father and ignore what I have said. The Inferno, it will have its way, no matter which you choose."

Okay. Okay, he could handle this. Of course he could. After all, he and Kat were planning to become engaged. Inferno condition sort of met, right? Maybe enough to skate by? "I plan to become engaged to her. That takes care of The Inferno problem, I assume?"

Primo inclined his head. "If you marry her, yes."

"And if we don't marry?"

His grandfather replied with a silent shrug, one that seemed almost ominous.

"What does it matter whether or not we marry? Married or engaged, I plan to end our relationship as soon as this Inferno runs its course," Gabe informed his grandfather. Or was it more in nature of a warning?

"Excellent."

Gabe's brows shot upward. "Really? I'm surprised you agree."

Primo shrugged. "If you wait until The Inferno runs its course, you have a very long wait. Nonna and I, we have been married for sixty years and I am still waiting for The Inferno to run its course. I am sure it will not last very much longer. Maybe next year my palm, it will stop itching, yes?" He shot Gabe a wicked grin from around his cigar. "Then again… Maybe not."

Kat despised her public dates with Gabe, though she did her best to hide her reaction behind a calm, remote façade. Christmas hung in the air, just two short weeks away. It scented everything with cedar and cinnamon, and danced in every store window. Santa and his reindeer, along with stylized Christmas trees, and pretty winter scenes decorated the outside of colorful packages slung over shoppers' arms, clear evidence of the seasonal spending spree. Despite that, she hadn't quite found her Christmas spirit. Maybe it had something to do with how painful her dates with Gabe had become.

Even after more than three weeks and a dozen or so similar engagements, their arrival at any given venue never failed to stir a wave of interest. Kat hoped the attention would rouse a response from her grandmother. Approval. Disapproval. Something. But so far, she'd remained pointedly silent, neither phoning nor responding to calls. At least Kat had been able to confirm that Matilda's silence wasn't a result of her illness.

The fascinated whispers followed them to their table, one that couldn't have been more centrally located if they sat on a spotlighted dais. This is what she'd experienced after the scandal with senatorial candidate Benson Winters broke. The avid attention. The nasty comments, made just loud enough for her to hear. The press hounding her. The shame and embarrassment. It had marked her, leaving painful scars, even after five full years, just as it had ruined Benson's shot at a Senate seat. Of course, the scandal had only been part of the reason, the other being the tell-all book his ex-wife released immediately afterward.

Gabe bared his teeth in a parody of a smile. "If you don't stop looking at me as though I were a meal you regret ordering, people will never believe we're falling in love."

"We're not falling in love."

"No, we're not," he agreed. For some reason the promptness of his reply hurt. "But we're attempting to convince others that we're not just falling, but have fallen deeply, passionately, madly in love. At the very least, a smile would be an excellent place to start."

"Fine." She made an effort to relax and smile. "Maybe if we exchange normal, casual conversation it will help."

"Anything is worth a try if it means you stop looking at me like you're on the verge of bolting." He tilted his head to one side. "How about this… Tell me about your time in Europe. Where did you live? What did you do?"

Okay, that was more comfortable ground, at least for the most part. "I lived in Italy, Florence to be exact. I worked as a barista, among several other jobs, and attended school."

"What were you studying?"

"Jewelry design."

So much for comfortable ground. For some reason her response caused Gabe's expression to close over. It figured. It would seem they couldn't even manage casual conversation. The only time the two of them experienced any sort of accord was in each other's arms.

"Jewelry design," he repeated.

"For two years." His reaction caused her to proceed with caution. She tiptoed a tiny bit deeper into the conversational landmine. "Then I apprenticed for the next three, determined to learn as much as I could in order to have a shot at working for the best of the best."

"And who do you consider the best of the best?" he asked softly.

For some reason, she stiffened, going on high alert. She couldn't explain it, her reaction was so immediate and visceral. One minute she saw a normal, rational male sitting across from her. The next she saw a fierce predator, ready to rip her to shreds at the first wrong word. "Dantes." And there it was. The wrong word. She broke into hurried speech. "I fell in love with Heart's Desire years ago, was always begging Gam to show me her necklace. I wanted to learn how to create jewelry just like it. From…from the best." She trailed off. "What's wrong, Gabe?" Because something was wrong. Terribly wrong.

He stared at her through narrowed eyes, as though attempting to see all she kept hidden from him. "An interesting coincidence, that's all."

"What's an interesting coincidence?" She hesitated, then asked, "Does this have something to do with your necklace?"

Instead of answering her question, he changed the subject. "What do you say we leave the restaurant, find the nearest bed and get naked? Maybe then we can establish a workable connection."

The total non sequitur caught her off guard and it took her a split second to recover her balance. Heat flooded through her and—if she were being brutally honest—so did blatant hunger. "I have no intention of leaving the restaurant and finding the nearest bed, let alone getting naked," she informed him, inordinately pleased with the crispness of her tone.

Granted, her voice tripped a bit over that last word, tripped enough that she reached for her coffee cup, changing her mind the instant she saw the telltale tremor of her fingers. Instead, she folded her hands in her lap and rubbed at an itch centered in her palm. For some reason it had been driving her crazy over the past few weeks.

Gabe shrugged. "Fine. If you're not hungry for food, we can always get the hell out of here and spend our lunch consummating our agreement."

Of course, she wanted to do just that. She wanted to consummate with every fiber of her being. Her toes curled in her Fendi slings at the very suggestion. She simply did not plan to follow through on her base desires. Still… If only he hadn't used that particular word. No, not consummate, although that sent her respiratory system into overdrive, as well. The one he'd used earlier. *Naked.*

That single word thrust amazing images into her head. Shocking images. Images she had no business painting, especially in such vibrant, glorious colors. It was wrong, wrong, wrong. Not that all that wrongness changed a damn thing. More than anything in the world, she wanted to see Gabe Moretti naked. Then she wanted his lovely nakedness poured over and into her like warm, creamy butter. She snatched up her cup—trembling fingers be damned—and buried her nose in the steam rising from the coffee, praying the warmth sweeping across her face would be attributed to heat, rather than sheer, unadulterated lust. No such luck.

His laugh held a dark richness that also reminded her of butter. "What *are* you thinking, Ms. Malloy? Whatever it is, it's gotten you all hot and bothered."

She kept her attention focused on her coffee. "It's irritation. Having to pretend to want you irritates me."

His laugh grew. Deepened. "Liar. You can't even look at me. I wonder why? Could it be that you're not pretending, that you really do want me?" He leaned forward and took the cup from her, setting it aside. He laced his fingers with hers so their palms bumped together. Somehow the bubbling heat intensified from a low simmer to just shy of a rolling boil. "I have no objection to skipping the foreplay and getting straight to the consummating, if that's what you prefer."

Four

Kat's gaze snapped to Gabe's. Big mistake. Huge. Desire flooded through her, throbbing with painful insistence, making it nearly impossible to force out a laugh, though she gave it her best shot. "Leaving the restaurant, finding a bed and stripping off our clothes is your idea of foreplay?"

His slow smile threatened to melt her into a puddle of molten desire. Where had her cool and calm gone, let alone her collected? Straight into that puddle of lava, if she didn't miss her guess. The waiter arrived just then and placed their orders in front of them. To her intense disappointment, Gabe released her hand. How was it possible that something so ridiculously simple as his withdrawing his touch could stir such an intense sensation of loss? She really was losing it.

He waited until they were alone again before responding. "Yes, getting the hell out of this place, sweeping you off to the apartment above my office—which conveniently has a bed—and stripping you out of that elegant, though unnecessary dress, is my idea of foreplay. Allow me to explain."

Kat drew a deep breath. *Focus, woman. And great, big postscript... Not on sex!* "This I have to hear."

He leaned toward her and lowered his voice. "Once we're done picking at our food—because who can eat when all we can think about is—"

"Consummating?" she inserted dryly.

"Exactly. We wait for the bill to come. Anyone watching can tell we're impatient to leave. We can't keep our hands off each other. Nothing overt, of course. Just glancing brushes. Little strokes and caresses."

Palms bumping.

Kat set her coffee aside and deliberately folded her hands in her lap. "Funny. My hands have informed me they're perfectly happy right where they are."

"They're lying." He lifted an eyebrow. "I can prove it, if you'd like."

Kat shrugged. "You can try. And you can fail."

That last comment might have been a mistake. Gabe's eyes brightened, flashing with a wicked light. "Ah, a challenge."

"That's not what I—"

"Too late to take it back now. I accept."

"But, I—" She glared at him. Okay, how bad could it get? They sat at a table in a public venue, with countless diners and staff looking on. They were both properly dressed and coiffed. Unless he planned to dump her on top of her *moules marinères* and have his wicked way with her, she was quite safe. How hard would it be to resist his brand of foreplay? "Fine. Do your worst."

His smile returned, slow and seductive. Uh-oh. Maybe she shouldn't have said that. He reached for her fork and scooped a mussel from its shell, offering it to her. As much as she wanted to refuse, she couldn't bring herself to do it in front of a roomful of diners. Determined not to be seduced, she accepted the bite. The flavor burst across her tongue while his gaze locked onto her lips so that she could almost feel his mouth on hers. For some reason, the cream, butter and garlic became spiced with the memory of his kisses.

"That's not fair," she complained.

"Tempted, sweetheart?"

If she were the type to pout, which she most definitely was not, she would have pouted. "Only for more mussels."

"What a terrible liar you are. You just don't want to admit that I'm seducing you in a restaurant. That everyone watching knows precisely what I want to do to you. What you're hoping I'll do to you."

Her lashes swept downward. "I have no idea what you're talking about."

He didn't bother arguing the point. Instead, he proved it by taking her hand in his once again and stroking his index finger in a tantalizing circle around her palm. A palm that itched and throbbed, and had ever since the first time he'd touched her. How did he know? She'd never considered her hand particularly sensitive before. But ever since meeting him… His index finger stroked her palm and every bone in her body liquefied. If he didn't stop, she'd end up sliding under the table where she'd let him consummate their deal. Several times.

Kat shuddered, well aware that her expression revealed every amoral thought and desire. "I can't believe this. Why you? Why now? I mean, this is insane."

"Agreed. Not that it changes anything." He tilted his head to one side. "Are you ready to concede that I win the first round?"

"Only if you agree it ends here."

Clearly, he didn't like the sound of that. "Explain."

She wanted him more than she'd wanted any other man she'd ever met. But there were lines she refused to cross. Lines she'd drawn to protect herself from the sort of pain she'd experienced five years ago. Lines that were an indelible part of who and what she'd become as a result of all she'd been through.

Kat released a sigh. "I don't want to go to bed with you. I won't sleep with anyone until I'm married."

"It's that important to you?"

She nodded, picking at her food, just as he'd predicted. For some reason, her appetite had evaporated. "Yes, it is."

"Why?" he demanded in abject frustration.

Kat hesitated, shrugged. "I won't have sex with you because—whether you believe me or not—it's who I am."

"And you think we can ignore this…?"

Gabe took her hand for the third time, lacing their fingers so their palms mated, one to the other. Heat flared, flashing from his hand to hers and she barely controlled the shudder that threatened to rip her apart. What the hell was that? Where did it come from? Why had it happened? Why Gabe Moretti of all people, when he was the last person in the entire universe she should sleep with?

She attempted to tug her hand free, to escape whatever held them, bound them. But he refused to let go. She closed her eyes, battling the wash of emotions that poured through her. "What is that?" she demanded between gritted teeth.

"The Inferno, or so I've been told."

"I don't understand. What is The Inferno?"

"Desire. Need. Lust."

She looked at him, even though she knew her look told him far too much. "Please," she whispered, not above begging. "Let me go." To her everlasting relief, he did so. She dragged air into her lungs, and sat back in her chair, her spine a rigid line. But at least she could think straight again. Somewhat. "I still don't understand."

"A restaurant isn't the best place for this conversation." He fished out his wallet, removed a couple sizeable bills and tossed them onto the table. "Let's go."

"Go where?" It was a foolish question. She knew. She knew precisely what he wanted and where he intended to take her.

"Anywhere with a bed," he said, confirming her suspicion.

Oh, God. If he attempted to take her to bed, she'd surrender to him...and he knew it, agreement be damned. Indelible lines be damned. Both of them damned by this churning, endless, inescapable want. All he had to do was touch her and she lost all ability to think straight. All he had to do was kiss her and she found herself on her back with her clothing half removed, offering herself like the sort of woman he believed her to be.

"Gabe, you promised."

"No, I didn't. I'm not sure I'm capable of making such a promise. I always believed I could control this sort of thing." A muscle in his jaw tightened. "Now I'm not so sure. But I do promise to try."

He held out his hand. Aware of all eyes on them, she took it, allowing him to draw her from the table and assist her with her coat. Unfortunately, no one else thought they would try to control themselves. They already saw the fall, an inevitable one. Amused whispers escorted them toward the exit. They almost made it to the door when disaster struck. The hostess led a party into the dining room, two women and two men. One of the men paused and caught her hand in his, spinning her around.

"Kat? Kat Malloy? Is that you?"

She paused, startled. "Benson?" Oh, no. Of all the people

to run into, today of all days. And in front of so many witnesses, all still watching with avid interest. She regarded him warily, not quite sure what to expect. When the scandal broke he'd loudly declared his innocence and had insisted she set him up, claiming he'd expected to find Jessa in the suite, not Kat. That she'd attempted to trick him in an effort to seduce her cousin's fiancé. Not that anyone believed him, any more than they believed her, especially once his ex-wife's tell-all hit the stores. "How are you?" seemed the safest comment to make.

He didn't appear to notice anything amiss. He was a tall, gorgeous man, hovering within shouting distance of forty, his blond hair, brilliant blue eyes and rugged build clear evidence of his Norwegian ancestry. The smile he aimed at Kat held both charm and sincerity. "I had no idea you were back in town. If I had I would have called." He gave her hand a squeeze. "I need to talk to you when you have a free moment. There's something I'd like to say. Will you call my office so we can arrange a convenient time to get together?"

Gabe came to stand directly behind Kat, resting a possessive hand on her shoulder. "Winters," he said, his voice as cold as the man's name.

Benson glanced at him, a wrinkle of confusion ridging his brow before clearing as he made the connection. His smile faded. "Moretti, isn't it?"

"Yes." His gaze settled on Kat's hand, still held in Winters'. "I strongly recommend you let go of my fiancée." Silence settled over the dining room at his comment.

Benson instantly released Kat. "Sorry, I didn't realize…" He frowned. "Did you say *fiancée?*"

Kat stepped free of Gabe's hold and turned to face him. "What are you talking about?"

"I'm talking about our engagement."

"There is no engagement."

"Yet," he corrected. "There is no engagement, yet. That's where we were going." He spoke to her, but the full power of those tawny eyes remained focused on Winters. "To discuss our engagement before I carry you off to bed."

His comment seemed to echo across the room. Kat closed her eyes, praying the earth would open beneath her feet and simply swallow her whole. No such luck. The silence stretched. Benson finally broke it with a quick laugh. "Well, congratulations, Moretti. You picked a real winner this time."

Kat caught her breath in dismay. They needed to leave, now, before that little shot struck home. She offered Benson a brilliant smile, slipped her arm through Gabe's and made tracks for the exit. They had just swung through the heavy wood and glass doors when the words impacted, slapping at him with the same harshness as the brisk, late December wind sweeping through the city's cement canyons.

"This time?" Gabe's eyes caught fire and he attempted to do a swift one-eighty. Kat clung to him and forcibly ushered him away from the restaurant. "What the bloody hell did he mean, *this time?*"

Damn, damn, damn. "Nothing. I'm sure he didn't mean anything by it."

"The hell he didn't."

"I'm sure it was just a figure of speech."

"It wasn't Jessa's fault their engagement ended."

No. Full blame rested on Kat and Benson's heads, or so Gabe believed, especially after witnessing the affectionate interaction between the "guilty" parties. His beloved Jessa was the innocent victim, whose name and reputation he'd protect at all costs. It was a battle Kat couldn't win, not here and now—or anywhere else, for that matter. So instead, she towed Gabe down the sidewalk and past the beautifully decorated storefront windows dressed in Christmas attire,

biting her tongue the entire way. She could only hope he
didn't force the issue and return to the restaurant to insist
Benson explain the crack. The faint strands of "Silver Bells"
slipped from a nearby department store, along with a crowd
of laughing customers. Maybe it would have a soothing influence on Gabe's subconscious.

"Bastard," he muttered. So much for a soothing influence.

"Let it go." Kat scrambled for a way to divert the conversation. "We were going somewhere private so you could
explain this Inferno thing to me, remember?"

To her relief, she succeeded in distracting him. "No, we
were going somewhere private so I could seduce you. Or,
attempt to seduce you."

"No, thank you," she said politely.

He shot her a grim smile. "You can try to say no, but I
don't think either of us are having much luck with that."

"No seducing." *Please. Please seduce me.* No! No, she
didn't mean to think that. Ever. "Maybe we should discuss
the engagement you just announced."

"That will definitely be one of the topics under discussion afterward."

"Afterward?" A full-blown picture erupted in her mind
of the two of them curled together, gasping out their sexual
release, his parts so entwined with her parts they were almost impossible to distinguish. Between her crazed imagination and her grip on Gabe's arm, happy signals flooded
prime areas of her body, areas that hadn't known any happiness in a very long time. She hastened to release him and
step away, a bitter-cold chill settling into the gap. "There
will be no afterward because there won't be a beforeward.
There will only be a discussion, and that held at a distance.
A safe distance."

"Again, we can try." He scratched the palm of his right
hand as though attempting to ease an itch centered there.

"Not sure it'll work considering The Inferno's 'unsafety' perimeter extends to at least San Francisco without any signs of diminishing."

She didn't quite get the San Francisco comment, but the way he scratched his palm was all too familiar. She'd been doing the exact same thing. And near as she could trace it back, the itch began at his Medina home when he'd first taken her hand in his and set off that bizarre burn that raced from her palm, straight through to the core of her. What the hell was going on? Somehow he'd contaminated her. Infected her with whatever infected him. She struggled not to scratch at her palm, too. One way or another she intended to get answers, though perhaps not in the middle of a bustling, downtown sidewalk, with the Christmas rush swirling around them.

"You are aware you've informed a key segment of Seattle we're engaged to be married after just three weeks of dating," she thought to mention.

Gabe stopped mid-step and scrubbed his hands over his face. "I did, didn't I? What the hell was I thinking?"

"I have no clue." She reached for his arm, catching herself at the last second. Best not to touch the pretty, sexy man again or let him touch her. Last time he did, she found herself flat on her back, decadently splayed, displayed and turned into a tasty appetizer. "Gabe, no one is going to believe we decided to get married after such a brief acquaintance."

He continued toward their destination, forcing her to keep up or be left standing in the middle of the sidewalk. "We wanted people talking." He shrugged. "This will do it."

"True, though I suspect the sort of talk they'll be exchanging won't work in our favor."

He opened the door to his office building and ushered her inside. Nodding to the receptionist, he headed for the elevators. "Let's go upstairs and discuss how we want to handle this. Come up with a game plan."

The elevator doors slid open and Kat stepped inside. "How about this for a game plan… How about you stop telling people we're engaged until we actually are?"

Gabe stabbed the button for the appropriate floor. "And how about you stay away from Benson Winters?"

The non sequitur threw her off balance. "Really? I mean, *really?*" *Oh, great comeback, Kat.*

"Considering the man put one hundred percent of the blame on you for your affair—told the media you tricked him into coming to that hotel room—he seemed pretty damned friendly today. Why is that, I wonder? Not that it takes much thought or imagination. It's clear to me that he was lying through his shiny white teeth about being innocent and tried to throw you under the bus to salvage his run at the Senate. No one could be that friendly toward a woman who totally screwed over his life. I guarantee he doesn't greet his ex-wife the way he did you."

"Maybe because she wrote that tell-all," Kat shot back. "That alone would have put paid to his bid for the Senate, even if we hadn't been accused of having an affair."

He turned to confront her, taking up far too much of an elevator car that seemed to be shrinking by the second. He even seemed to be using up too much of the air, taking far more than his fair share. "So, I repeat. Stay the hell away from the man. I won't have your ex-lovers ending our engagement before it's even started."

Fury ripped through her. "How, in any way, shape or form is that meeting my fault? It was sheer coincidence that we bumped into him. And just for the record? He's *not* my ex-lover."

"Bull. I know the truth, Kat. I was married to Jessa, remember? She gave me chapter and verse about you and

Winters. Not to mention what I witnessed with my own two eyes." Heat rolled off him, raising the temperature in the close confines of the elevator. "Nor do I believe in coincidences, not when it comes to you two."

"Well, start. Because that's all it was." She didn't bother addressing his comment about Jessa. What was the point? He'd never believe her. Instead, she planted her hands on her hips, fighting to remain cool and calm. She didn't bother with composed this time. She didn't have a hope of attaining it. "And FYI? We're likely to run into him again in the future. He may not be a senator, but he is a renowned businessman who will undoubtedly receive invitations to some of those high profile events you want us attending. In fact, I'm shocked we haven't run into him before this."

He took a step in her direction, leaning in. He towered over her, despite the added inches her high heels afforded. Everything about him exuded pure masculine strength, lethal in its ability to devastate every one of her defenses. Beneath his anger she caught a surge of hunger, a silent roar of need that tugged at her, stirring an answering need.

"I don't want you talking to him," Gabe insisted. "It defeats the entire purpose of our engagement."

"Do you think I don't get that? I'm not stupid," she informed him. "I understand precisely what sort of threat Benson poses. Just like I get your need to stake your claim, to warn other males away from what you regard as your property. Well, newsflash, Moretti. I'm not your property."

"Yet," he snapped. "You're not my property. *Yet.* I'm sure you understand how important it is to change that small detail from perception to fact. Which is why I need to do this…"

He fisted his hands in the collar of her wool coat and yanked her onto her toes. Then he took her mouth in a kiss that exhilarated every bit as much as it devastated. The emotions she'd attempted to hold at bay crashed down on her, swamping thought and reason and all inclinations but one. Consummation. Now. She wrapped her arms around Gabe's neck and thrust her fingers deep into his hair, dragging him closer. Then she opened to him, gave him everything she possessed before taking with a demanding greed that left him groaning in pleasure.

His hold shifted from her coat to cup her face, tilting her head to give him better access to her mouth. Butter. He really was like butter, melting on her and over her and in her. She felt her knot of hair loosen and slide down her back, and couldn't help laughing against his mouth. She didn't understand why he always tugged her hair free, but for some reason he didn't like it confined. He shoved her coat from her shoulders, leaving it to pool at her feet. Then he was kissing her again, the demand growing with each passing second, the blistering heat inching toward unbearable levels.

Kat had no idea what might have happened—though she had a nasty suspicion it involved the floor of the elevator and the emergency stop button—if the subtle ding warning that the doors were about to open hadn't brought her to her senses. With a soft gasp, she yanked herself free of his arms an instant before the doors parted, leaving her the most exposed and vulnerable she'd felt since being discovered naked in Benson Winters' hotel room.

Gabe swore beneath his breath and swiftly stepped in front of Kat to block the scrutiny of an elderly woman who stood near the elevator doors, clearly about to enter. Neither woman had recognized the other—yet. With luck, the few extra seconds he could provide Kat would give her time to recover her poise.

"Matilda, this is a surprise." He leaned against the elevator doors to hold them open, blocking the interior of the car with his broad shoulders. Behind him he heard a swift, horrified gasp. "If you're here to see me, your timing is perfect."

As always, Matilda dressed impeccably. A silk Italian scarf in a wash of ocean blues accentuated eyes the soft turquoise of a Caribbean sea, while her winter-white wool suit provided a stunning complement to hair of the same shade. "I'm here to determine whether or not the rumors I've heard are true. I can scarcely credit they are."

"That depends on what you've heard."

He'd given Kat as much time as he could. Turning, he swept her coat from the floor of the elevator and fit his hand to the small of her back. He ushered her from the elevator car, careful to act as a solid bulwark separating the two women.

"Katerina!" Based on Matilda's shocked look, she hadn't noticed her granddaughter until that moment. Equally apparent was her abrupt and profound awareness of what Kat and Gabe had been doing during their elevator ride. She took a wobbly step backward and Gabe caught her arm in order to steady her. Her gaze flashed from him to her granddaughter, a certain desperate intensity lurking in her expression. "Then it's true? The two of you are involved?"

Even more gut-wrenching than Matilda's reaction was Kat's expression. The utter devastation and bittersweet longing with which she regarded her grandmother threatened to tear Gabe apart. "Gam," she whispered, and he could practically hear her heart break over that single word.

Once again, they were the center of all eyes. "Why don't we continue this discussion in my office?" he suggested.

The instant they were closeted behind the heavy barrier of his oak door, he assisted Matilda into a chair in the sitting area near the wet bar. "I have brandy." He gave Kat a subtle jerk of his head. "It's in the decanter on the left. Would you pour your grandmother a small glass?"

"Thank you," Matilda murmured. "I'd appreciate that."

To his surprise, Kat hesitated. "Your doctor won't object? It's safe for you to have a drink?"

Matilda stiffened and to Gabe's surprise she, too, hesitated. Her gaze flitted to the windows just over his shoulder, fixing on the wintery sky, laden with dark, heavy rain clouds. "At this point, it hardly matters," she said, and shivered. "I can feel the cold all the way to my bones. To be honest, I could use a small sip of brandy."

He took a seat across from her, studying her closely, examining her for any changes in the six months since he'd last run into her. It had been at an art exhibit for a small museum where she served as docent. She seemed more tired in comparison, a bit frailer, perhaps. But her gaze still burned with a power that defied the weaknesses of old age. Keen intelligence glittered there, while strength and experience lined a face more handsome than beautiful. And yet, he could also see the vulnerability, a perfect match to her granddaughter's.

"I'm sorry to hear you haven't been well," he told her.

"That's a polite way of putting it."

"It's serious, then."

She lifted her shoulder in a dismissive shrug and smiled calmly. "Does it matter? After all, life is a terminal illness, isn't it? From the moment we're born, we march inevitably toward death. It just comes down to when."

Crystal chattered in jarring disagreement. "Sorry," Kat murmured. "I seem to be all thumbs today. Must be the cold." She approached, offering her grandmother a small snifter of pale brown brandy, tinged with the tiniest hint of red.

For a moment their gazes locked and Gabe could feel the tension vibrating between them. He could see the words bottled between them, words neither dared speak for fear of what might escape. The risk of what might be said—or the even greater risk of what remained unsaid. And yet it hovered there, darkening the air with painful emotions, still unresolved. Of accusations and declarations. Of regret and recrimination.

But most intense of all was the helpless yearning emanating from Kat. The way she reached for her grandmother, the offer of brandy as intimate as a touch. And he saw something similar in Matilda's expression, in the gentle manner in which she took the snifter, the unnecessary brushing of hands during the exchange. The way they both attempted to make the lingering of fingertips look pragmatic and detached when everything about them brimmed with intense emotion and need.

Then the moment passed, never to be recaptured, leaving the words unspoken and the emotions tightly contained. Matilda sipped her brandy and Kat returned to the wet bar to pour two more drinks. He noticed she poured herself a double, and accepted the tumbler she offered. No lingering of fingertips with him. And there sure as hell weren't any soulful gazes. Deliberately, he caught her hand in his and pulled her down beside him before turning his attention to her grandmother.

"So, what brings you out on such a cold, blustery day, Matilda?"

She didn't answer right away, but simply regarded them over the rim of her snifter, taking in the way he held Kat's hand. "I already told you. I came to discover the truth. Now I can see for myself that you are involved."

"Gam, please," Kat whispered.

Gabe wasn't quite sure whether she was asking for permission or approval, or perhaps was offering an apology.

But Matilda ignored her, keeping her gaze fixed on him, instead. "Is it serious?"

"We're engaged," he replied gently.

"That seems rather sudden."

"It is," he agreed. "But when it's right, it's right."

Now she did spare Kat a look and he realized why she'd ignored her granddaughter up to this point. She was afraid. Afraid she'd shatter if she spoke to Kat directly. Sure enough, she turned back to him, holding on by a thread. "You're engaged, despite what happened five years ago? Despite what she did to Jessa?"

He waited a beat, then shrugged. "Jessa and I never would have married if it hadn't happened. She'd have married Benson Winters instead."

"Perhaps," Matilda surprised him by whispering, heavy doubt underscoring that single word. Her fingers tightened around the brandy snifter, blanching white beneath the pressure. "I should tell you I always hoped you'd marry my granddaughter. Once upon a time I thought I would try my hand at matchmaking. It seemed to offer such nice symmetry when it came to Heart's Desire. But…" She shrugged. "Events got in the way."

Intrigued, he asked, "You were going to try your hand at matchmaking with me and Jessa?"

Matilda shook her head. "Not Jessa. Kat. It was always my intention to give her Heart's Desire."

Kat jerked in surprise and Gabe chose his response with care. "Well, as it turns out, you were right, though no matchmaking needed, apparently."

A ghost of a smile touched Matilda's lips. "Yes, I can see that. It's all worked out on its own. I'm relieved since Kat loved that necklace from the day she first set eyes on it." Her gaze flickered in Kat's direction, clung, then shifted back to Gabe. "I suspect it's part of the fabric of who she is. I also suspect it's part of the fabric of who she's become."

The observation gave him an odd jolt. Heart's Desire was also part of the fabric of who he was and who he'd become, and he couldn't help but wonder how the cloth that formed his life compared to Kat's. "Why not just sell the necklace to me, outright?"

"I have my reasons." Her tone sounded a shade defensive and she swept a hand through the air in clear dismissal. "Besides, now that you're engaged, it's no longer an issue. You'll have the necklace soon enough. At least, your wife will."

"Gam, the necklace belongs to Gabe," Kat broke in. "I have no objection if you sell it to him. As you say, once we're married, it won't matter, right?"

"I won't sell the necklace," Matilda retorted. "I don't need or want the money. I promised I'd leave it to you after I was gone, Katerina, and that's what I intend to do. I honor my promises, just as I taught you to do. What you choose to do with the necklace afterward is entirely your affair."

"Oh, Gam." Kat left his side and crouched at her grandmother's feet and dared to gather an arthritic hand in hers. "I don't want the necklace. I just want you. It's all I've ever wanted."

Tears glistened in Matilda's eyes. "I have my reasons for what I'm doing," she repeated. She caressed Kat's cheek with gentle fingers before her hand fell away. "But maybe…Yes, maybe there's a better way. Instead of leaving the necklace to you in my will, why don't I give it to you as a wedding present?"

It took every ounce of Gabe's self-control not to swear out loud while Kat shot a quick, panicked look at him from over her shoulder. "Matilda—" he began, though he suspected it was far too late.

Before he could say another word, she set her brandy

aside with a decisive click of crystal against wood. "Yes. Yes, this is the perfect alternative. A much happier alternative than a deathbed bequeath." She stood, tucking her handbag under her arm and adjusting her scarf. "When is the wedding?"

"We haven't—" Kat began, also standing.

"Soon," Gabe overrode her. "Very, very soon."

"Excellent. Sooner is better for me, all things considered." Matilda paused, and for the second time a heartbreaking vulnerability clung to her. "You…you will invite me once you've set a date?"

Kat spared Gabe a helpless look before nodding. "Of course. I wouldn't dream of getting married without you there."

Matilda gave a brisk nod. She took a single step in Kat's direction before catching herself, but Gabe could see the effort at restraint fighting the longing to make amends with her only surviving grandchild. Kat's chin trembled and then set in a slant remarkably similar to her grandmother's. She deliberately stepped forward and enclosed Matilda in a tight hug. Only Gabe saw the anguish mirrored on both women's faces. And then the moment ended and Matilda walked from his office, her spine set in a rigid line.

Kat turned blindly in his direction. It wasn't until she focused on him that the realization hit her. She caught her breath in a silent gasp. "Oh, Gabe. If she won't give us the necklace until we're married, what are we going to do now?"

He laughed, the sound without humor. Did she have any doubt? "You know damn well what we're going to do. We're going to marry."

Five

Kat shook her head. "No. No, we can't." A hint of her earlier panic swept through her words. "I'll talk to Gam. I'll convince her to give us the necklace for an engagement present, instead."

Gabe lifted an eyebrow. "You think she'd agree?"

She hesitated, and he could see her debating whether or not to answer honestly. "Probably not," she finally confessed. "But it's worth a try. I just don't understand why she's so set on giving it away instead of selling it."

"Something else you can ask her. And something else she can refuse to explain."

Kat's shoulders sagged. "I'm sorry, Gabe. You know it was never my intention for everything to get this far out of hand. We don't have to marry. We can string out the engagement until—" She broke off, her breath quickening. "Until after Gam is gone."

"She looked remarkably spry for someone on her deathbed."

Kat flinched. "Please."

He tilted his head to one side, studying her. "You were serious about the reason you proposed this ludicrous agreement. This really is all about Matilda, isn't it?"

"Yes." Fire flashed in her pale green eyes. "I told you I'd do anything to reconcile with her and I meant it."

"Even to the extent of marrying me?"

She nodded. "If there's no other option." It was her turn to study him. "I gather that means you're equally determined to get your hands on Heart's Desire?"

"I'll do whatever it takes." He took a step in her direction and tugged her into his arms, reveling in the helpless heat of her body against his. "Kat, it symbolizes love, a love that went hideously wrong. Of a love that started with a single touch."

"The Inferno?"

"The Inferno," he confirmed.

She frowned, splaying her hands against his chest. "You were going to explain that to me. Explain what The Inferno is and how it works."

"It'll be clearer if I demonstrate."

And then he did.

Kat's lips were like silk, yet sweet and a shade tentative. For some reason her hesitation drew Gabe in, made him desperate to break through her reserve and have her surrender to him. To give him everything she possessed without holding back. He didn't want to storm her defenses the way he had in the elevator. This time, he wanted it to be her choice. This time, she would acknowledge the uncontrollable desire that gathered them up in a whirlwind of need and exploded into The Inferno. It was the only way to make her understand what was happening between them.

He sensed her teetering on the edge, trembling on the brink of letting go. It would only take one little nudge and she'd tumble once again. He nibbled at those lush lips, teasing them apart. With the softest of moans, she opened to him. And still he held back, silently demanding she choose. She could admit that she wanted him or she could step away. But he refused to force the decision, refused to have her accuse him later of taking advantage of the passion that seared all senses and destroyed all sensibility.

He kept his arms loose around her, so she could back away any time she chose. Instead of pulling free, she snuggled closer, pressing those impressive curves tight against him. Her hands slid up his chest and around his neck, skating into his hair. He didn't know how much longer he could hold on, his need almost painful in its intensity.

"Gabe, please."

Just those two little words, barely audible, yet ripe with longing. And then he felt the give of her body, the sweet yielding of years' worth of defenses. His arms tightened, molded her against him, sealing her to him. They didn't rush, but slowed. Didn't feast, but savored. Immersed themselves in the heat, inch by delectable inch, instead of throwing themselves onto the pyre.

Not that it made any difference. The need built, just as it had from the moment they'd first touched. Soon it would overwhelm. For some reason Gabe didn't want that to happen this time. Instead, he wanted to simply flow with her, testing the newness and delighting in the discovery of what made her different. Special.

The one.

Those two simple words crashed down on him, the weight of all they suggested as heavy and overwhelming as the urge that demanded he take Kat in every way possible. He allowed the kiss to ease, to soften, to ever so tenderly end, before he pulled back and rested his forehead against hers.

Why her? Of all the women with whom he could have shared this instant connection, why did it have to be Kat Malloy? It was a betrayal of all he believed. All he held dear. Of his late wife, Jessa. Of the clear-cut lines he'd drawn in order to overcome his past and separate himself from the man who'd sired him, as well as the taint of his Dante heritage. Instead, that heritage had connected him to the last woman he would have chosen and stirred emotions he'd never thought himself capable of experiencing.

She wasn't the one. He didn't want her to be. As for The Inferno... Gabe refused to accept his grandfather's claims that he would be forever mated to this woman, heart and soul, for the rest of his life. He controlled his own destiny, chose whether to turn left or right. Chose how he conducted his affairs, both business and personal. Chose whom he permitted into his life and for how long. Though he'd allow Kat access, it sure as hell wouldn't be forever. Not after the way she'd betrayed his late wife. Just holding her, wanting her, this uncontrollable drive to possess her in every conceivable way, felt like another betrayal, one of the worst sort. And yet...

He couldn't resist this woman.

She stared up at him, her eyes shrouded in bewilderment. "You stopped. How could you stop when I—"

Couldn't? Was that what she'd intended to say? Her breath escaped a shade too fast and rich color suffused her cheekbones. It took her several seconds to pull herself together. "You confuse me. You really do."

"You asked me to explain The Inferno. I thought a personal demonstration would clarify what it is far better than any number of words."

It was the first thought to enter his mind and he went

with it. He released her and took a step back, allowing cool, rational thought to chill the primal heat seething between them. It helped, but nowhere near as much as he'd like. Unable to resist, he touched her again, stroking the back of his hand along the soft curve of her cheek. She shuddered. And he wanted. No. That struck him as too innocuous a word. He didn't simply want. He yearned. He craved. Every fiber of his being demanded he take her in order to fill the ravenous hunger clawing at him. And he resisted that hunger with every fiber of his being, knowing all the while he resisted the inevitable. This woman would be his. It was only a matter of time.

His hand lingered on her skin, drew a scorching line from cheek to jaw. "This… This is The Inferno," he murmured. "Or so I presume."

Kat leaned into Gabe's touch, seeming to draw comfort from the contact. "Well, I've heard it called many things, but Inferno is a new one on me."

He continued to paint her face with his fingertips, searing each curve and angle into his memory. "It's what the Dantes call it."

She stilled, her expression closing over. This time she stepped away from him. "The Dantes. You mentioned them before. Do you mean the Dantes who designed your mother's necklace? The same company I hope to work for someday?"

"Yes." He didn't want to have to discuss them, but didn't see any other option. "I'm related to them."

She turned from him ever so slightly, withdrawing even more. He felt the loss and almost reached for her, catching himself at the last instant. "I didn't realize."

He shrugged. "Very few know. It's not something I often discuss."

"You've lost me." She wrapped her arms around her waist. It seemed a telling gesture but Gabe couldn't quite hone in on why it concerned him. "Why would you keep your con-nection to them a secret?" she asked.

"Because it's not one I care to acknowledge." She re-mained silent and he sensed she was waiting for him to de-cide whether to say more or simply end the conversation. For some reason, he felt compelled to explain. "My mother had an affair with Dominic Dante. At the time of my con-ception—a very married Dominic Dante."

A small frown touched her brow and he wondered whether his bastard status bothered her, whether she would change her mind about marrying him now that she knew. "And the family has never accepted you?" Then she soft-ened, taking a step in his direction. "Oh, Gabe, I'm so sorry. That's just wrong."

And once again, he'd misjudged her. Her concern for him couldn't have been any clearer. He read it in her eyes, heard it in the tone of her voice, felt it in the quick, spontaneous squeeze she gave his arm.

"Until recently, the Dantes didn't realize my sister and I existed. To be honest, they still don't know about her," he continued.

She gave him an odd look. "Sister?" She shook her head, not bothering to hide her confusion. "Wait a minute. You have a sister?"

"Lucia. We're twins." Was that hurt he caught flickering across her expression? Why? It wasn't as if they were close friends. Hell, the only place they experienced any sort of closeness was in each other's arms. "There's no reason you should have known, Kat. You were out of the country when Jessa and I married, which was the only time you could have met Lucia. And over the past three weeks, you and I have been careful to avoid intimate conversations in case it led to other intimacies. Although I expect that will change in the near future."

Kat blew out a sigh. "And I thought I kept my cards close to my chest." She scooped her hair back from her face and Gabe suppressed a grin at the irritation flitting across her expression. She always kept herself so carefully put together, wearing her cool, remote façade like a suit of armor. He liked the idea of stripping her of that armor, bit by bit, and seeing what hid beneath. "Why don't you start from the top?" she suggested.

"My mother was a jewelry designer at Dantes and had an affair with Dominic. When he married someone else, she transferred to their New York office. They met again years later and had a one-night stand that resulted in our conception. When she discovered she was pregnant, she left the company to work for Charlestons, a then-competitor, before moving to Seattle about the time we were born."

"Did Dominic know your mother was pregnant?"

"No, not then. Eventually, he tracked her down and found out about Lucia and me. It was right before our sixteenth birthday." Memories swamped him of his father, an older, larger version of himself, with a charm that made him almost irresistible. At least, he'd proved himself irresistible to two members of his family. After watching his mother pine for his father for so many years, Gabe had been less enchanted by the arrival of the Dante "prince." But his sister... "Lucia was thrilled. She bought into the whole fairy tale gig. The prince was going to marry the princess and carry us all off to his San Francisco castle where we'd be one big, happy family."

"Since your last name is Moretti, I assume that never happened."

Gabe shook his head. "And who knows if it ever would have. A few months later, my father died in a sailing accident, along with his wife. His death destroyed my mother."

"And Lucia?"

Compassion underscored her question, a compassion he itched to openly reject. "It left scars," he replied. He thought about Lucia's current job working for Primo, and the naked longing he'd seen in her expression. "Some still haven't healed."

"But you never bought into the fairy tale, did you?"

It was a shrewd guess. "Never. I'm not a Dante. I'll never be a Dante."

"Except for one small detail," she mentioned.

"Which is?"

"The Inferno." A hint of exasperation colored her words. "You keep saying this Inferno business comes from the Dantes. So, what is it, exactly?"

They'd come full circle, an irony that didn't escape him. "The Inferno is an infection. Or perhaps an affliction." He stared at his palm and ran his thumb across the surface. The tingle remained, the slight burning itch he'd experienced ever since first touching Kat. For some reason it seemed to intensify the desire that never left him, that constantly gnawed at him, demanding he allow himself to be consumed by the flames of what this hellish Inferno had sparked. "Or, more likely, another fairy tale."

She groaned. "Do I really have to drag it out of you?"

He took a deep breath and got to the point. "According to my grandfather—" Suddenly realizing what he'd said, and the fact that it caused Kat to raise an eyebrow, Gabe grimaced. "Technically, he is my grandfather."

"I didn't say a word."

"You sure thought a load of them." He waved off her attempt to respond and let her have it. All of it. "According to Primo, the Dantes can tell their soul mate with a single touch."

She held up her hand, palm out, a frown tugging at her brow. "That touch? The one that caused my palm to burn?"

"Yes. They call it The Inferno."

Her frown deepened, not that he could blame her. "How long does it last?"

He simply looked at her before dropping a single, shocking word between them. "Forever."

"For—" Kat's mouth fell open and she sank into the nearest chair. "You've got to be kidding."

"I didn't say it was real. I'm just telling you what my grand—*Primo*—said. It's another fairy tale," Gabe emphasized. "Just some silly family legend. But since I'm not a Dante, it doesn't apply. Not that it would, even if I were a Dante." Frustration ate at him, and bled into his voice. "Damn it, Kat. It's not real, okay?"

"A legend," she repeated. She shot him a look from blazing eyes. "As in, this story has been around for generations. Usually legends which have been around that long have some basis in reality."

"Right, reality." He couldn't keep the cynicism from creeping into his voice. "Let's examine the reality of this particular legend. Two strangers touch for the first time and instantly know they belong together for the rest of their lives. That's what you want me to accept as 'real'?"

She scrambled for an explanation. "That, or some version of it. More likely some version, like a chemical reaction when a Dante touches a woman they're attracted to. Maybe Dantes have more acidic skin, or more basic, or their skin contains an excess of some chemical that others don't normally possess. I mean, how should I know?" She closed her mouth and snatched a quick, steadying breath. "So, seriously. How long does this thing last?"

"I told you. According to Primo, it lasts forever."

"And according to you?"

"I figure it'll take a few months to work out of our systems." He offered a cool smile totally at odds with the heat smoldering within. "About the length of our marriage, I'm guessing, assuming we move forward with our devil's bargain."

He caught that hint of vulnerability he'd witnessed during their first meeting. Now, as then, it unsettled him on some visceral level. He didn't want to believe it genuine. She'd had an affair with a man engaged to her cousin, whereas his mother had slept with a married man. He'd never blamed his mother for that affair, had understood that she'd been helpless to resist his father. Had Kat felt that way about Benson Winters? How could he condemn one, but not the other?

"You believe that if we sleep together this Inferno will burn itself out?" she asked, that hint of vulnerability continuing to twist something he kept buried deep inside.

"Yes."

Her lashes swept downward. "And if it doesn't?"

"It will." He reached for her, lifted her out of the chair and pulled her into his arms. In that moment he realized he didn't give a damn about her past, only her immediate future. And what the hell did that say about him? Maybe that he was more his father's son than he cared to admit. "Don't think for one minute that whatever we're experiencing, whether Inferno or chemical reaction, is going anywhere. It's lust, Kat. A simple hormonal or pheromone response. You want me and I want you. End of story."

"An itch?"

"Exactly. We scratch it and after a while it goes away."

"Just like that."

Gabe couldn't help smiling at the snap in her voice. "You're offended."

"I guess I am," she admitted. She lowered her gaze for a moment before looking at him again, her expression reflecting an unwavering determination. "I don't like being compared to an itch. Nor do I appreciate being made to feel like a case of poison oak you'd like to cure at your earliest convenience. And I certainly don't intend to sleep with you in order to take care of your little problem."

"You want me."

To his surprise, she nodded, not backing away from the truth. "I'd be lying if I said I didn't. But that's not enough for me. It never has been. It's not who I am."

"So you were in love with Benson Winters?" He found the idea unsettling in the extreme.

"Not at all."

His eyes narrowed. "That was an aberration? Or are you telling me your affair changed you?" He put the final two words in air quotes, which might have been a mistake based on the flash of anger that swept across her face. "That you've learned your lesson and will never again allow yourself to be drawn into an affair to satisfy an itch?"

"I don't owe you an explanation for what happened with Benson," she informed him crisply. "It's none of your business."

"It is if we marry."

"No, Gabe. It's not." She stepped away from him. "You and I have a business arrangement, pure and simple. That's all it is. For some reason we've allowed physical desire to sidetrack us. But I, for one, don't intend to make that mistake again. This isn't about lust, or sex or even The Inferno. Our relationship is about Heart's Desire and my reconciling with my grandmother. That's it."

The reminder brought him up short. "And just how do you plan to prevent us from getting sidetracked again?"

"I don't plan to prevent it. I plan to ignore it," she stated simply.

Yeah, right. Look how well that had worked so far. "And I've explained why that's not possible," he retorted. "You want your reputation restored so your grandmother will accept you. I want Heart's Desire. To get what each of us wants, we're stuck with a long-term engagement at the very least, possibly even a marriage. It's already strange enough that I would marry you—of all people—after what happened between you, Winters and Jessa. You don't want to give anyone additional reasons to peek behind the curtain, particularly not your grandmother."

"You want the world to believe we're lovers? Fine. We'll just have to do an impressive job faking it." She gathered up her purse. "Thank you for lunch, Gabe. It was…interesting. I'll be in touch tomorrow. Maybe we can coordinate our calendars and pencil in some more lunches and dinners and that sort of thing. Dates." She edged toward the exit. "Public dates that are, well, conducted in public. Where we don't need to be alone. Ever."

"Sure." He stopped her retreat with a hand to her arm. "One quick thing before you go?"

She paused. Lifted one of those elegant eyebrows. "Yes?"

"Just this…"

He didn't give her any warning. He simply wrapped his arms around her and pulled her close. He waited just long enough for her to open her mouth in protest before sealing it with his own. He sank in, mating her tongue with his, telling her without words that her plan to conduct a celibate marriage had a snowball's chance in hell of succeeding. She silently argued the point for an entire ten seconds before conceding defeat.

She fell into the embrace. No, that suggested something far too passive. A surrender. She didn't surrender so much as a single inch. Instead, she attacked, gave as much as she took. Her tongue swept inward with a swift, sweet thrust, dueling with his. He savored her taste all over again, finding it just as delicious as before. She gave his bottom lip a quick nip, then soothed it with a gentle caress.

All the while her clever hands tripped across his body
in open exploration, pausing to wander over the ridging of
his chest, before gliding around him to trace the hard planes
of his back. She wrapped him up tight while she consumed
him, her breasts full and heavy against him, while her hips
moved in tiny, urgent circles that threatened to drive him
insane with the need to take her. And still those restless
hands couldn't seem to settle, never quite satisfied until
they finally slipped back to his chest and arrowed downward, skating past his belt buckle to cradle the heavy weight
of his erection.

For some reason she froze, as though she'd found far
more than she'd bargained for. Okay, fine. That just meant
it was his turn to do a bit of exploration. He found the zipper
to the Christmas-red dress she'd painted on and dragged it
downward, allowing his fingertips to follow the path of her
spine to the sweet indent just above her backside. He slid a
single finger along the lacy elastic band of her panties and
felt her shudder in helpless reaction.

"Gabe, please." The words escaped in a helpless moan.

"Please stop?" he teased. "Or Gabe, if you stop I'll have
to hurt you."

"Yes, that one. The stop and I'll have to hurt you option."

His laugh escaped, deep and intimate and filled with dark
promise. "That's what I thought."

More than anything, he wanted to strip away her clothes
and simply drive into her, right then and there. But with
his office door providing no more than a flimsy barrier between them and the outside world, he didn't dare. Combine
that with the fact that he didn't keep condoms in his office
and it added up to right time, wrong place. He snatched another kiss, intending only a quick taste before releasing her.
Somehow it deepened, drifted from one moment into the
next. If he didn't find a way to get her to his office apart-

ment—and fast—he really would say to hell with it and
spread her across his desk in order to seal their commitment to one another.

Forcing himself to end the kiss, a heroic effort considering how desperately she struggled to prolong it, he wrapped
an arm around her and ushered her toward a staircase at
the far end of the sitting area. The climb to the penthouse
seemed endless. She hesitated at the top of the stairs, and
stared at the large, sprawling apartment. Floor-to-ceiling
windows showcased a stunning sweep of Seattle and the
Bay, before wrapping around to encompass Mt. Rainier. The
snow-covered peak loomed over the city, making one of its
startling appearances against the mid-December skyline.

For some reason, she eased back a pace, shaking her
head. She clutched her loosened dress tight against her chest.
"No, not here."

Her abrupt turnaround caught him by surprise. "What's
wrong, Kat?"

"Not here," she repeated. "Not where Jessa…"

He understood then. "Jessa never stepped foot in this
apartment. I didn't even own this office building when we
were married. I purchased it more than a year after she died."

Kat closed her eyes in relief, her breath escaping in a soft
laugh. "I guess it seems ridiculous to you."

"Not at all." For some reason he was driven to reassure
her. "I only use this place when I've been working late and
rather not face the drive home. If it makes you feel any
better, I've never made love to a woman here before. Any
woman."

"Keeping business separate from personal?"

She left the question hanging between them and stepped
away, crossing to stand in the flood of sunshine arrow-
ing through the windows. She rubbed her arms as though
chilled. Of course, that might have something to do with her

dress gaping open in the back, exposing the lovely width of her shoulders, the endless expanse of flawless skin that curved inward to a narrow waist he could encircle with two hands before flaring into shapely hips. It always came as a shock to realize how petite she was, perhaps because she had such a huge personality. Well, that and the mile-high heels giving her the illusion of height. Gabe came up behind and wrapped his arms around her, tucking her against the warmth of his chest.

She relaxed into him, her head settling into the crook of his shoulder. "I guess since, technically, I fall under the heading of business, they're still separate."

He bent his head, his mouth brushing her temple. "Just to clarify, I've put together hundreds of business deals over the course of my career. Not one of them involved what we're about to do."

He felt a laugh ripple through her. "I have to admit I'm relieved." She turned to face him, her hands resting against his chest. "Gabe…"

And there was that defenselessness again, that gut-churning uncertainty that brought out every last protective instinct he possessed. He'd always been the protective one in his family, the one who stood in front of his mother and sister and attempted to absorb the blows aimed their way. Not that he'd succeeded. But at least he'd been there for them every step of the way. He should protect Kat, too. Maybe he would have, if the need to have her didn't override all instinct except one. And that instinct demanded he join them in the most basic and elemental way possible, a mating that had bound man to woman since the beginning of time.

"Don't," he urged. "Don't back out. Not now. Not when you know damn well what we're about to do is inevitable. Whether it happens today or tomorrow or next week or next month, it will happen."

"We've only known each other a matter of weeks. That's no time at all," she protested.

"If ours were a normal arrangement, I'd agree with you. But it isn't. Not only are the circumstances—well, frankly—bizarre. But so is our reaction to one another." He captured her chin, the soft curve centered in the palm of his hand directly over The Inferno's burn. "Tell me the truth, Kat. Have you ever experienced anything like this before?"

She didn't hesitate. "Not even close. But that doesn't mean we have to jump into the fire."

"Too late. The fire's already jumped into us. All we can do is let it consume us."

He saw it first in her crystalline green eyes, the quiet acceptance. "I didn't plan this."

"I know. Neither did I."

Her gaze never wavered. "I also know if you could have picked someone to experience The Inferno with, I'm the very last one you'd have chosen."

He didn't deny it. Couldn't. "I suspect, if we were honest with each other, we'd have both chosen someone else. But it doesn't change the fact that it's happened. We can deny it. We can try to ignore it. We can fight it. And yet, here we are, unable to resist going where The Inferno leads."

"Damn Dantes," she whispered.

He laughed. "Now there we're in total agreement." His amusement faded. "So, what's your decision, Kat? Do you continue to deny it? Keep fighting? Ignore whatever the hell this is? Or do you surrender to the flames?"

Her smile held a bittersweet quality. "I think that decision has already been made, don't you?"

"You're killing me, Kat. I haven't even touched you—not really. Not the way I intend to. And you're already experiencing regrets."

"Only because this is going to change everything."

He didn't disagree. How could he when it was the truth? "Nothing about this situation is easy."

He expected tears, but he didn't see any hint of them. And he couldn't help remembering her claim that she never cried. Ever. Instead, sorrow lurked in her light green eyes. For some reason the pain it hinted at impacted far harder than it should have, than even tears would have. He shouldn't care. Didn't want to care. And yet, in that moment, if he could fix whatever had hurt her, he would have.

"According to my grandmother, the Chatsworth family excels at difficult," she said with a lightness that missed its mark. "I'd hoped our association would prove the exception to the rule."

Gabe shook his head. "I'm not easy. Neither are you. And our history pours more turmoil onto an already tumultuous relationship."

"Sleeping together won't make our relationship any less tumultuous," she pointed out.

He shrugged. "I think The Inferno has already made certain of that."

She nodded and with that simple inclination of her head, he knew she'd made her decision. She stepped closer, the sun caressing the sparks of fire buried in the darkness of her hair and intensifying the bright red tones of her dress. She lowered her hands to her sides and gave a graceful shrug. The dress slipped from her shoulders and drifted downward to settle at her hips. He'd expected to see her wearing black undergarments again. But she wasn't. These were a creamy white, delicate and virginal and sweetly feminine, at total odds with the sophisticated dress she wore.

She gave a rolling shimmy of her hips and the dress took a long, slow slide to her feet. She stepped from the pool of silk and slipped off her heels before approaching. When had she become so tiny? And when had her appearance changed to mirror her undergarments—delicate and virginal and sweetly feminine? It was an illusion. It had to be. But it was an illusion that filled Gabe with a burning desire. To take her. To brand her with his possession. To be the one. The first, the last. The only. He surrendered to the fantasy, knowing full well that's all it was. A fantasy. Soon enough reality would intrude. But until it did…

He reached for her and she swept his hands aside. She didn't want him to touch her? Fine. He'd play by her rules. For now. She came to him and tugged at the knot of his tie, sliding it from around his collar and tossing it aside. Next, she pulled his shirt free from his trousers and worked her way down the row of buttons. Her hands spread across his chest, sculpting the warm, lightly furred skin, trailing her fingertips in agonizing circles downward across the ridge of muscles. She made short work of opening his belt and unzipping his trousers. And then she stripped him, saving his boxers for last.

Instead of removing them, as well, she turned and gave the apartment a cursory look, settling on the doorway leading to the bedroom. She headed that way, the high cut of her panties exposing buttocks that were round and lush and as bitable as ripe, white peaches. She paused at the threshold of the bedroom to give him a single glance over her shoulder. Her hair spilled over her shoulders like dark flames, licking across the creaminess of her shoulders and cupping the sweet curve of her breasts. She was the goddess of temptation, personified. And he couldn't help recalling that Até was also the Greek goddess of folly and despair, that she'd caused the downfall of many a man, usually through his own hubris.

How incredibly fitting.

Then she said, "Coming?" in a voice that made promises that nearly brought him to his knees.

Six

That's all it took, just that single, sultry word. Coming? Oh, hell yes, he was coming. Gabe made a sound from somewhere deep inside, from the very core of him. It was part growl, part exclamation. But it was wholly a claiming, a statement of sheer, masculine possession.

He went after her, charging across the room. He never slowed, simply scooped Kat into his arms and entered the darkened bedroom. In two seconds flat he had her tossed onto the bed, pale, silken limbs splayed across the bronze duvet. Her hair framed her face, and her lovely, sculpted features fought to appear impassive. Yet they revealed their secrets to anyone who bothered to look—really look. Vulnerability lurked in the forest-draped shadows of her eyes, while passion sculpted her lush mouth. Hesitation softened the lines of a determined chin, at direct odds with the urgency revealed by the taut planes of her cheekbones.

He came down beside her, tracing a fingertip from eyes to mouth, chin to cheekbone. "So much conflict."

"Is that what you see?" she whispered. "Is that all you see?"

"You want me."

"True."

"But you don't want to want me."

Her mouth trembled into a smile. "Also true."

"I guess that pretty much defines our relationship."

Her eyes fluttered closed and her breath came in a soundless sigh. "Are you trying to talk me out of this?"

Hell, no! Still… "I don't want any regrets afterward. No recriminations about not waiting until there's a ring on your finger." he replied, surprised by how gentle he sounded. For some reason she brought that quality out in him. "I'm trying to be honest, Kat."

Her lashes flickered back upward and she gave him a calm, direct look. "Not here. Not now."

Her comment surprised him and he lifted an eyebrow. "You want me to lie to you?"

"I want to say yes, lie to me." She caught her lower lip between her teeth, thinking about it. Then she sighed. "But, I'm afraid that would be a mistake," she admitted reluctantly.

He couldn't blame her. After all, he wanted the fantasy over reality, too. "Tell you what… Why don't we focus on the 'want' instead of the 'don't want.'"

"I'd like that very much." But instead of reaching for him, she levered herself up onto her elbows. "What do you say we also make a bargain?"

He groaned, not sure whether to laugh or strangle her. "*Another* negotiation?"

"Just a small one." She pinched two fingers together in demonstration. "I think the one thing we both can agree on is that we want each other sexually. As you said, we may have fought it, but if we're dead honest, we'll admit we can't resist the physical desire we're experiencing."

"I can't argue with that."

"So, let's take that one step further. Instead of lying about what we want, what if we agree that this is the one place we'll always be honest with one another? The one place where, no matter how painful, we won't lie?"

"Naked."

She nodded. "In every sense of the word."

He leaned across her and opened the drawer of the night-stand table and removed one of the condoms he'd only started keeping there these past three weeks. Had he been hoping this moment would come...or planning? He tossed the foil packet onto the bed beside them so it would be within easy reach when the time came. Without another word, he cupped her face and kissed her, telling her loud and clear just how much he honestly wanted her and how little the "don't want" factored into the equation. Her lips parted and their tongues began a teasing parry. Her kisses were divine, lei-surely and playful.

But it wasn't enough. Not nearly enough.

There was so much more he wanted from her. So much more he wanted to offer her. Desperation filled him, a nearly uncontrollable urge to strip away the flimsy bits of silk and lace covering her and mate their bodies in one swift, hard taking. But something held him back. Maybe it was those scraps of innocent white, with their tiny feminine bows dec-orating the deep cleft between the cups of her bra. More bows perched on the flare of her hips, looking adorably sweet on a woman who epitomized European sophistication. The dichotomy gave him pause, as did the nervous tension that exuded from her.

After a moment's consideration, he decided to go with his instincts. This was their first time together. There would be plenty of occasions for faster, more exuberant encounters. But this afternoon, he'd take his time. Build toward that ultimate peak, slow caress by slow caress. Kiss every inch of that delectable body. And he'd begin with the soft, sweet center. Always a delicious place to start.

He lowered his head and pressed a string of kisses across the warm sweep of her abdomen, inhaling her feminine perfume. She shuddered in surprise and arched her spine a few inches. He smiled against her stomach, pleased to catch her off guard. He planned to keep her that way. She was a woman who liked to be in control. Well, not here. Not now. He wanted to devastate every last defense and have her fully participating, without any controls. With total loss of control.

He stroked her sides, his fingers teasing at the bows riding her hips. He felt the slight quiver of her belly beneath his mouth, the brief tensing in anticipation of his stripping away her panties. Instead, he skated upward to trace the contours of her bra. Again, he felt the shudder of reaction, the uncertainty and confusion he'd roused.

"Gabe, what are you doing?" she finally gasped.

"Playing." He lifted his head to look at her. "I can't seem to decide which ride I want to go on first."

She froze, clearly not expecting his levity. Apparently sex had always been serious business for her. Sad, really, when it was so much damn fun. Then she chuckled, relaxing against his hold. "Playing, huh?" She planted her hands on his chest and allowed her palms to rumble downward across his abdomen. "I think I'll go for the roller coaster."

He cupped her breasts and pressed them together within the confines of her bra. "I've always been rather partial to the bumper cars."

She allowed her gaze to drift downward and settle at the telltale bulge pressing against his shorts. "Somehow I thought you'd go for the sledgehammer. I bet you ring the bell every time."

"For you, I'll do my best." He teased the tiny triangle covering her womanhood. "Shall we start with the Tunnel of Love, or end there?"

She wrapped her arms around his neck and tugged him into her embrace. He fit against her, perfectly melded, male to female. His key to her lock. "Start there. End there. So long as you ring my bell along the way, I'm willing to go on every ride there is."

He smiled to see how much their silliness had relaxed her, how comfortably she settled against him. How the faded rose of the afternoon sun painted her in carefree colors. The worries that had burdened her melted away and she lingered in the moment, safe within his arms, within his bed and within their growing rapture. He could read the pleasure in her pale green eyes, see it in the happy tremble of her mouth, hear it in the laughter that had become part of their first sexual encounter. He reveled in it all, shutting out the darkness, along with the past. None of that mattered. Not here. Not now.

They made a game of stripping away the last of their clothes, of exploring one another's bodies. There was a sweetness to their teasing, a gentleness that permeated voice and comment and touch. And yet, all the while, tension built, the flicker of need lurking behind the lightheartedness they both knew would eventually explode into flames and sweep like wildfire into their encounter. Despite their awareness, it caught them both by surprise when it finally happened. One moment they were laughing at how he'd turned her body into an arcade game, and the next…

Gabe stilled, the laughter easing, dying. Vanishing. A ray of sunshine flickered across Kat. Winter gave the light a soft, remote quality, framing her in that softness and attempting to paint her into someone distant and untouchable. But it couldn't. She possessed too much vibrancy, her coloring streaked with touch-me passion rather than touch-me-not pastels.

Heaven help him, but she was beautiful. Fire crackled in her hair and seemed to catch in the earthy green of her eyes. A smile hovered on her lips, easing from amusement to a womanly perception. Eve becoming. She reached up to cup his face and he felt the slight tremble of her fingers. He turned his face into the palm of her hand, pressed his lips to the center where The Inferno first struck.

Now when he traced her body, he did it with intent, putting into practice what he'd learned while playing. She was extra sensitive right around the nipples and on the bottom slope of her breasts, and he lingered there until she trembled in his arms, the breath hitching in her throat. He'd also discovered she shuddered in ecstasy whenever his fingertips skated along the back of her thighs, that desire cascaded off her and she instinctively opened to him whenever he touched her there. He found if he tugged at her lower lip, taking it in a gentle love bite, she'd plunder his mouth with uncontrolled urgency. She was self-conscious about her backside, considering it too generous, though he found her bottom about as perfect as a bottom could be. And the kisses he placed on the little dimples just above all that lushness drove her insane.

Inch by inch, he explored each and every part of her, determined to build the fire into a conflagration that would be unlike any she'd ever experienced before. He drove her ever upward until he realized that he hovered on the brink every bit as much as she did.

He snatched up the condom and handed it to her. "Put it on me," he said. "I want to feel your hands on me."

It took her three tries to tear open the foil packet. And she had him teetering on the edge of control with the slow, teasing way she went about the task. First, she pretended to get the angle wrong, then claimed she'd tried to put it on inside out, before finally sheathing him, slowly unrolling it until he couldn't take it another second.

He lowered himself on top of her, poised at the warm, moist heart of her. "Wait, Gabe," she whispered, pushing against his shoulders. "I don't think I did it right."

"No more teasing," he told her. "Not now."

"But—"

He stopped her protest with a slow kiss and thrust inward, breaching the tightness at the same instant he breached her mouth. She stiffened, squirming against him in a way that almost had him finishing before he'd started. He gathered himself, determined to bring her as much pleasure as she brought him. Slowly, he pulled back, before driving into her, burying himself deep within. There he paused, though he thought it just might kill him, waiting for her to become accustomed to the joining. And all the while, he found those areas that gave her the most pleasure. Her stiffness eased, melting away, and her arms tightened around him. She opened more fully to him, lifting upward, searching for a rhythm.

It amused him that they weren't instantly coordinated. He'd have thought that two fairly experienced people would get it together a little faster than they were. But maybe that was The Inferno's fault. Maybe the urges that swamped them, that threatened to overwhelm them, were so intense they didn't allow for expertise, just gratification in the fastest, most basic way possible. Then the rhythm caught, amplified, became something he'd never experienced before, something that sank inward and connected on a level he didn't realize existed. It transcended all that came before, sang into the now, and made promises for what would come in the fullness of time. He saw the burgeoning of whatever seed had been planted reflected in Kat's eyes, saw that same connection.

Then something changed.

She bowed upward, her gaze locked on his, filled with shock and disbelief. Filled with innocent delight. "What have you done to me?" The words escaped in a thready whisper. And then tears filled her eyes, tears she'd denied possessing. They slid down her temples and burrowed into the dark embers of her hair, glittering with the rawness and purity of rare fire diamonds.

And then she came utterly undone, her climax slamming through her. It drove him straight over the edge and he fell. Fell hard.

Fell into innocence.

Gabe turned from the window and stared at Kat. Late afternoon sunshine splashed across her sleeping form. Another image transposed over the current one, an image of how she'd looked in Benson Winters' hotel bed. But the image was all wrong. It tilted. Fractured. Splintered into pieces that would never be whole again. She hadn't been Sleeping Beauty after the awakening. The Sleeping Beauty from five years ago had never known the prince's kiss…or anything else.

It explained a lot about their lovemaking, including the way she'd fumbled with the condom. She hadn't been teasing, dragging out the moment in order to increase his pleasure. She'd been inexperienced and attempting to conceal it from him. It also explained why she'd wanted to wait until they were married, something he'd denied her.

He lowered his head. He'd been the one to push, to insist they make love here and now. The image of her looking at him in response, her haunting, haunted eyes filled with quiet acceptance cut deep, as did the memory of her bittersweet smile. Other images came to him, deepening the cut. Her reaction when she'd thought he'd brought her to a bed Jessa might have shared with him. Those damn virginal undergarments. Even her surprise at his playfulness in bed. Why hadn't he seen? Why hadn't he understood? Why hadn't he protected her, if only from himself? He'd been the one to awaken her, and now that he knew what to look for, he could see the difference. Feel the difference.

What he'd assumed was fantasy had been reality. And if that were true, then it also meant that reality was… Well, not what he'd assumed, he knew that much for damn sure.

That still didn't explain how she'd ended up in that hotel room bed all those years ago. Could Winters have been right? Had Kat attempted to seduce him that night? No, that didn't make sense. Unless he was complicit in that seduction, he'd never have greeted her so warmly at lunch. Nor would he have asked to meet with her again. Gabe thought it through, attempting to use the dispassionate logic that had aided him throughout his life. But somehow he couldn't remove himself from his emotions. Not this time. Not when it came to Kat.

There were any number of explanations for her virginity, including… An image came to mind, of Jessa arriving on his doorstep in tears, begging him to go with her to a hotel room where she'd been told she'd find her fiancé in bed with another woman. At that point he'd been no more than a friend. After they'd found Kat, his relationship with Jessa had swiftly become something more. He turned from the memory, unwilling to examine that particular possibility. Which brought him back to the woman currently gracing his bed.

One thing he knew for certain. His was the only bed Kat had ever been in. And his was the only bed she'd be in for a long time to come. He retreated to the living area and retrieved his cell phone from his trousers. The series of calls didn't take long. The one to Primo met with delight and instant approval, the one to Matilda met with almost identical enthusiasm. After that, it came down to simple pragmatism—arranging for the flight, the hotel rooms, the necessary license. Amazing what money and connections could accomplish in such a short span of time. Once finished, he returned to the bedroom—and to the bed.

Gabe eased down beside Kat, warming her with his body, gathering her within the shelter of his embrace. In sleep her barriers were nonexistent, her vulnerability sculpted into every line of her body. He swept a tumble of hair from her face and leaned in, wakening her with a slow, passionate kiss. She moaned softly, still half-asleep, opening to him. Giving herself without restraint or hesitation. Gifting herself.

Her lashes fluttered and she opened her eyes, dark and slumberous and edged with passion. "Is it morning?" she asked, her voice blurred and husky.

"Dusk."

She laughed softly. "I'll never sleep tonight."

He swept a lock of hair from her face. "I can think of a few things we can do instead," he gently teased.

"I don't doubt it."

Ah, there she was. Not gone at all. The prickly defiance, the dry irony, it just hadn't fully awakened. "We need to talk."

She stiffened, regarding him with a familiar wariness. "About what?"

"Let's see… Life. Death. Taxes." He paused a beat. "The fact you were a virgin. Explain that to me, Kat."

He had to hand it to her. Even though warm color swept across her cheekbones, she continued to fix him with a direct gaze, not so much as blinking. "I'd really rather not explain anything."

"I'd really rather you did." He unleashed a hint of steel. "In fact, I'm afraid I must insist. And since you were the one to bargain for honesty when we're in bed together..."

"Damn it." She glared at him. "Bed Honesty was supposed to work in *my* favor, not yours."

Bed Honesty? He would have laughed if it weren't so painfully serious. "Yes, most unfortunate. For you." He hooked her chin and tilted it into the wash of fading sunlight. It stripped through artifice and laid her bare. "How is it possible that you were having an affair with Winters and yet came to my bed untouched?"

She shrugged. "It's a miracle?"

"Or, you weren't having an affair with Winters."

"That's certainly another possibility." She led with defiance. It bled into every part of her from expression, to voice, to the rigid tension of her body. "You may recall I did tell everyone at the time."

"And no one believed you." He fought against the impact of that, along with his own culpability. But it wasn't easy, not when he'd contributed the most to her condemnation.

"The evidence was rather damning," she conceded.

"Winters claimed you tried to seduce him."

"Yes."

"But if that were the case, why was he so friendly toward you at the restaurant?" That single question continued to nag at him.

"Maybe he realized I'd been set up."

"By whom?"

Her mouth tightened and emotions cascaded over her. Anger. Betrayal. Disappointment. Hurt. "You know who set me up, Gabe. You just don't want to believe it. No one did, not even my grandmother."

It struck him then that not once had Jessa intruded into his time with Kat. Not as a regret. Not as a comparison. Not even as a shard of guilt. But she swept between them now, like an unforgiving arctic wind, scouring the landscape— or in this case the bed and its occupants. "She was my wife. You're asking me to believe—"

"She wasn't your wife at the time," Kat cut in. "And I'm not asking you to believe anything. I don't give a damn what anyone believes or doesn't believe. I know what happened. I've lived with it for five years. I've lived with the condemnation, was called a whore. Accused of trying to steal my cousin's fiancé. Accused of wrecking Benson's reputation, not to mention his hopes for a Senate seat."

"I don't understand something, Kat. Why would Jessa set the two of you up? It doesn't make sense."

"What does it matter, Gabe? She can't tell us. And any explanation I might offer is sheer speculation. Not that it's any of your business."

"It is my business if Jessa's involved." He cupped Kat's cheek, his voice deepening. "And it is if you're involved. Because as of this moment, I'm involved, too."

She pulled free of his hold and escaped the bed, only to look around in bewilderment, no doubt wondering where she'd left her clothes. Giving up, she crossed to his closet and yanked out a chocolate-brown robe. She pulled it on and knotted the sash around her waist. It was miles too large, making her appear even more defenseless than when she'd been wearing nothing at all.

"I don't want to talk about it anymore," she announced, turning to face him.

"You mean, you don't want to tell me the truth. That's why you left the bed."

Kat glared at him, scooping her hair from her face with both hands. "Okay, fine. I don't want to tell you the truth— not that there's any great truth to reveal. Besides, it's not like we're married."

"That's about to change."

Wariness draped her more thoroughly than his robe. "What are you talking about?"

"I've made arrangements for us to fly to San Francisco. We leave first thing in the morning. I've already made arrangements to stop by Matilda's and pick her up. We can also swing by your hotel so you can pack a bag." He left the bed and approached, snagging the collar of his robe and reeling Kat in. "In two days' time, you will be my wife. And then we'll be returning to bed, at which point you will tell me what I want to know. Every last *honest* detail." He leaned in, his mouth a breath away from hers. "Even if it means keeping you there until you do."

And then he sealed his promise—or was it a threat?— with a kiss that had The Inferno erupting like Vesuvius, consuming them in endless heat.

Kat sat in a leather captain's chair of Gabe's corporate jet and stared out the small port window while they streaked toward San Francisco. He'd been so solicitous with Matilda, settling her into the small onboard bedroom after they were safely airborne in order to ensure she didn't get overly tired during the flight.

One thought occupied her above all others. How did Gabe know she'd been a virgin? The only possibility she could think of was that her lovemaking had been so amateurish and unskilled there hadn't been room for any other possibility. She cringed from the thought, especially when she considered how he'd shut down in the wake of that final, blistering kiss.

She'd hoped knowing the truth about her and Benson Winters would help their relationship. Instead, it did just the opposite. Gone was the playful man who'd taken her to bed. Gone was the passionate man who'd made her his.

Gone was even the tentative accord they'd struck in order to accomplish their joint goals. Instead, she faced a man she didn't know, a man so barricaded within himself that she had no idea how to break through to the Gabe who'd made her first sexual experience so shattering.

Even though every instinct urged her to protest the speed of their marriage, she didn't dare. After all, it was what they both wanted, even if it struck her as happening far too fast. She spared Gabe a swift glance. He'd buried himself in work, his face set in taut lines. Something was wrong, something more than the swiftness of their impending wedding. For some reason, he'd set himself on a course, refusing to waver from it.

So, what had happened to cause that fatalistic grimness to settle over him like some sort of dark shadow? Was it simply that she'd been a virgin? That didn't make sense. Granted, due to his history he tended to be protective. Maybe even overly protective. That still didn't explain the rush. Not really.

She shifted in her seat. Fine. If he wouldn't volunteer the information, she'd ask. And if that didn't work, she'd demand. And if *that* didn't work, well she'd just have to seduce it out of him. Drag him off to anyplace with a mattress and use their Bed Honesty agreement to force the truth from him. Did it make her a horrible person that she hoped he'd refuse to speak until the seducing and dragging commenced?

"Gabe, I wish you'd reconsider our marrying so quickly," she finally broke down and said. "No one will believe it's real. And I don't want Gam to suspect it's related to the necklace."

"She doesn't. Hell, Matilda and the Dantes already believe it's genuine. And soon, everyone else will follow suit."

"I don't understand," she pressed. "Why? Why are they

suddenly so quick to accept that it's real? And why will everyone else believe it, too? What's changed?"

He hesitated so long she didn't think he'd answer. Then he admitted, "What's changed is who I am. Once the media discovers I'm—" He broke off, a muscle jerking in his cheek. "Once they discover I'm a Dante and that we've been struck by The Inferno, they'll have no choice but to believe. Especially when my father's family steps forward to support the union."

He'd shocked her right down to her tiptoes. "You're going to tell people?" Why did the thought fill her with such apprehension? "I thought you didn't want anyone to find out about the connection. I thought you despised the Dantes."

"I do." He lifted his gaze to her, his eyes tarnished with bitterness. "But it will explain the speed of our marriage."

She didn't like this. Not his plan. Not how badly it seemed to impact him. And especially not how deeply it scored him on a personal level. "I still don't understand," she said uneasily. "How will announcing your relationship to them explain the rush and make it all acceptable? Why should it matter that we've experienced The Inferno? And more importantly, why do we have to rush into marriage instead of waiting a few months?"

He set aside his papers with a sigh. "I keep forgetting you've been out of the country for the past five years."

She regarded him in surprise. "Did something happen during that time that relates to all this?"

"The Inferno happened," he replied. "All this nonsense became public a few years ago when one of my father's sons, Marco, staged some sort of media event to prove his wife could tell him apart from his twin, even blindfolded, all thanks to The Inferno. It was reported in just about every scandal sheet out there, and even hit some of the more respected news sources. If I announce publically that I'm a

Dante, and admit we were struck by The Inferno when we first met, no one will question the speed or validity of our marriage, especially with a wall of Dantes at our back."

"The Dantes are going to support us in this?" If so, it could mean only one thing. He'd gone to them. He'd asked for a favor.

"Yes. That's why we're marrying in San Francisco, so the Dantes can publically throw the weight of their name behind us."

She understood then, both the cost and her own culpability. She'd gone to Gabe, been the one to suggest this insane engagement. And it had been her grandmother who'd put a potential marriage on the table by promising to give them Heart's Desire as a wedding gift. Her actions, as well as Matilda's, had put him in his current predicament, and her heart broke for him. He'd sacrificed himself for her. For their marriage. And she had the odd feeling it wasn't just for Heart's Desire. For some reason, his decision to move forward so rapidly and to involve the Dantes had to do with what happened between them in bed yesterday. She just had to uncover what, and more importantly, why the rush?

"Oh, Gabe," she whispered. "You didn't. You didn't go to the Dantes."

His mouth compressed. "It's the only way."

"No. It's *not* the only way. We can wait, just like we planned. Wait to see if Matilda won't change her mind." She leaned forward and touched his knee. "Gabe, please don't do this, not unless you're using it for an excuse to initiate some sort of reconciliation with your father's family."

He returned his attention to his papers, though he flipped through them far too fast to truly absorb what he read. "It's done, Kat," he stated with finality. "Besides, it's no big deal. I've simply arranged for the Dantes to support our marriage.

Best of all, there will be very little for us to do. Primo is taking care of most of the wedding details for us."

She struggled not to wince at his calm, indifferent tone. "Will your grandfather be attending?"

A short, harsh laugh escaped. "Oh, not just Primo. The entire family. You'll get to meet all the Dantes, all the ones who have denied my existence since the day I was born. And you'll get to know who and what I am. What I came from. What I reject." He regarded her grimly. "And most of all, what I'm grateful I never became."

She allowed the words to wash over her, to recede, realizing he was hellbent on this course of action and that nothing she said would cause him to deviate so much as a single step. Keeping her voice calm and pleasant, she asked, "Is Lucia attending? She's the one I'm most interested in getting to know."

His indifference vanished and he smiled with genuine affection. "Yes. You'll get to meet Lucia." His smile faded. "But I should warn you, she's working undercover for Primo. He doesn't know who she is and I want to keep it that way. I don't want her hurt again. She's been hurt enough for one lifetime."

So, protective. But then, she'd caught that same reaction each time he'd mentioned his mother and sister, and even at odd moments, toward her. "She's working for Primo? I'm surprised, especially after all you've told me about your past."

"It came as a surprise to me, too." Gabe shrugged. "I only found out recently."

Kat took a moment to consider, the answer obvious once she thought about it. "She wanted to get to know her grandfather, didn't she?"

"Yes."

She saw it then. The wound. The pain from what he perceived as a betrayal. His determination to conceal it. He was a lion with a thorn in his paw—perhaps one she could help excise. "I guess she doesn't share your feelings toward the Dantes," she commented idly.

Of course, he saw right through her. "Leave it alone, Kat."

She pressed a little harder, searching for the thorn and realizing it was buried deep. "You must have been hurt when you found out. It must have felt like a betrayal on some level."

"What part of 'leave it alone' didn't you understand?"

But she couldn't leave it alone. She decided to go in fast and yank hard. "Gabe, I'm sure Lucia wasn't trying to hurt you. Nor is she saying that you aren't enough. It's natural that she'd be curious about her father's family."

The thorn popped free, causing the lion to roar in reaction. Then he swiped at her, claws extended. "Let's see if this won't stop you from talking."

He heaved himself out of his seat and reached for her. Yanking her into his arms, he took her mouth in a hard, fierce kiss, allowing his anger free rein. If he thought it would intimidate her, he was mistaken. She gave him back kiss for kiss, making hers just as demanding as his. Dear heaven, but she wanted him, every bit as much now as before they'd made love. Maybe more, since she knew what to expect. Understood how it felt and what it did to her. To them both.

She dragged her mouth from his, pressing frantic kisses along his jaw line. "Gabe, please."

He groaned. "Please stop? Because I don't think I can."

"I don't want you to stop. I want you to make love to me."

"Make love," he repeated. He closed his eyes and leaned into her, simply holding her. "Don't call it that. I don't want to hurt you, but I will if you try to turn this into something it isn't. It's not love. It's sex."

"Or The Inferno?"

To her surprise, he didn't instantly deny it. Instead, he blew out a sigh. "What the hell does it matter what we call it? I just know it won't last. You need to understand that."

"What does that have to do with the speed of our marriage?" she asked uncertainly.

He glanced down at her and for the first time she saw a crack in his defenses. "Because I didn't stop when you asked me to," he replied cryptically.

She frowned in confusion. "I don't understand. I didn't ask you to stop."

His expression softened and he tucked a strand of loosened hair behind her ear. "The condom," he reminded her. "It came off, sweetheart. You told me you hadn't gotten it on right and tried to stop me. I thought you were teasing. But you weren't."

Her confusion turned to shock. "You think—" She broke off, struggling to breathe. "You think I'm *pregnant?*"

Seven

Gabe nodded. "Pregnancy is a serious possibility. So we marry sooner rather than later, particularly if you want to reconcile with your grandmother. You've only just begun to reestablish your relationship with her. I don't want my taking you to bed to sabotage that. Better she think we married because of The Inferno, than suspect it was a shotgun wedding."

The possibility wiped every single thought from Kat's head, but one. Pregnancy. A baby. Gabe's baby. The mere thought that she could be carrying his child made her lightheaded. Images flashed through her mind. A dark-haired son with eyes of liquid gold. A baby nursing at her breast. Gabe protectively cradling a child they'd created. Gabe, The Inferno burned out, caught in a trap of her making.

Oh, dear God. She couldn't do that to him.

Kat yanked free of his arms. "No. That's not possible. I'm not pregnant, not after just one mishap."

Instead of replying, Gabe simply lifted an eyebrow at the absurdity of her response.

"Okay, fine," she said. Her hands darted through her hair, destroying the sleek knot and finishing the job Gabe had started. "It's a possibility. But a remote one, right?"

"If you say so. I'm not willing to take the risk. We need to marry, anyway, if I'm to get my hands on Heart's Desire. This just put an expiration date on our engagement a little sooner than expected."

"How can there be an expiration date when we weren't actually engaged? I mean, it's not like you even proposed. Not really. In fact, I think I'm the one who did all the proposing." Aware her voice had risen, she snatched a deep breath, struggling to regain her self-control, an almost impossible task. Everything seemed to hit at once, overwhelming her. "Oh, Gabe. What are we going to do?"

"We're going to take it one step at a time."

She nodded, steadied by his calm response. "And the first step is getting married."

Gabe laughed, though she didn't catch so much as a trace of humor in the sound. "Wrong. The first step is dealing with the Dantes and the preparation for our wedding."

"And that's a bad thing?" she asked uncertainly.

He hesitated. "That's a complicated thing."

Kat quickly discovered just what he meant by that when they were met at the airport by a private car carrying Primo. He puffed on a fragrant cigar, releasing a tiny wreath of smoke that practically jittered with nerves. After being introduced to Matilda, he turned to Kat. The shock of his resemblance to Gabe dissolved beneath the enthusiasm of his European-style greeting, a tight hug and a kiss on each cheek. Fortunately, her years in Italy had accustomed her to the exuberance of many of its compatriots and she returned the embrace with a natural generosity.

"It's a pleasure to meet you," she told him.

"And you." He stepped back and held her at arm's length in order to get a good look at her. "So. You are Gabriel's Inferno mate. The Inferno has been most generous in its choice for my grandson."

Kat couldn't prevent a blush. "Thank you."

He glanced toward Gabe and grinned. "No greeting for your Primo?"

To Kat's surprise, Gabe stepped forward and embraced his grandfather. She could practically see Primo's nervousness evaporate beneath the hug. "Thank you for meeting us. And for taking care of the wedding details."

"It is my pleasure to do this for you. I welcome the opportunity." He slapped Gabe on the back. "Come. We go to meet Nonna."

Ah, complication number one, Kat realized. They were ushered toward the car, Primo insisting Matilda sit beside him with Gabe and Kat facing them. She was impressed with how gentle he was with her grandmother, teasing slightly, but always respectful, despite the fact that they were of a similar age. Maybe Gabe had warned his grandfather about her precarious health. At Matilda's insistence, they dropped her off at Le Premier. It didn't take them long to get her settled in her room before continuing on to Primo's home in Sausalito, working their way through the crowded city streets toward the Golden Gate Bridge.

"Who will be there?" Gabe asked abruptly.

Primo offered immediate reassurance. "It is only Nonna for now. We will not overwhelm you with all your many brothers and cousins, nieces and nephews until the ceremony. But I warn that your grandmamma is not happy about this meeting." He thumped his chest with his fist. "Not like your Primo, who is delighted to have you with your family where you belong. She is more like you, Gabriel. She is not certain she wishes to acknowledge the connection."

"Then why force it?" he asked, his voice stiff with pride.

"Because you are the son of my son," Primo answered simply. "You are also the son of her son. She will see this the moment she sets her eyes on you. She will see her son reborn in you and these reservations will vanish like the morning fog."

"I am not like Dominic," Gabe said, withdrawing into winter's embrace. "Nor will I become some sort of replacement for him."

"No," Primo replied with a hint of sadness. "This you will never be."

He turned his attention to the sights they passed, giving Kat a guided tour along the way. At long last, they reached the ferry terminal and trendy shops clustered near the harbor and took a winding road that zigzagged high into the hillside. The car dropped them off outside a large wooden gate of a spacious home overlooking Angel Island and Belvedere. Primo opened the gate and ushered them through to a large yard overrun with dormant gardens. Though they were held tight in the clutch of approaching winter, Kat could tell they'd be spectacular come spring. In place of flowers, someone had decorated with fairy lights, holly, Christmas wreaths and garlands.

"Welcome to my home." Pride blended with the flavor of Tuscany to accent Primo's voice. He gestured toward the decorations. "When it grows dark, it is quite beautiful. Not too much, not too little. Just right, *capito?*"

When Gabe remained stubbornly silent, Kat answered for them both. "I'm sure it's spectacular."

She glanced at the man who would soon become her husband, tempted to give him a swift elbow to the ribs, only to discover her mistake. He hadn't fallen silent due to rudeness, but out of respect. He fixed his full attention on a woman who sat at a wrought iron table beneath the protective embrace of a mush oak. With that single exchange, the two spoke volumes to one another and the atmosphere thickened with tension.

Primo followed Gabe's gaze and grinned, oblivious to the growing friction. "Ah, and there is Nonna, waiting for us with hot chocolate." He paused, beaming in delight. "Look, my boy. Is she not the most beautiful of women? Never have I seen anyone who can lighten my heart and make it dance with such joy. But then, you have discovered this with your Katerina, yes?"

Gabe replied by taking Kat's hand in his. "Your wife is beautiful, Primo." He glanced down at Kat, a hint of concern reflected in his gaze. "She also looks scared to death," he murmured beneath his breath. "When she's not glaring at me, that is."

"I'm sure you'll find a way to win her over, as well as reassure her," Kat replied softly. "To protect her from hurt."

His hand jerked in hers. "Protect her?" he repeated.

She couldn't help smiling. "Isn't that what you do? Isn't that what you've always done?"

"I've tried, but—"

"She's angry at her son, not you," Kat whispered. "And she's frightened because she doesn't know how to handle this situation. She's afraid you'll bring harm to her family. She just needs to know that you don't intend to hurt them. And you don't, do you?"

"That depends."

"Gabe… I know what it's like to lose my family, to be cut adrift and have no one. Absolutely no one. I would give anything to have my grandmother back in my life." The words seemed torn from her, filled with trembling passion and heartache. "You have that chance, right here and now. I'm begging you, don't let it slip by."

They didn't have an opportunity for further conversation. Primo ushered them forward. He must have picked up on the emotions swirling between his wife and grandson, and puffed nervously on his cigar in response. The instant Nonna's gaze arrowed in on it, he gave a choking groan and whipped the cigar from his mouth, burying it in the nearest mound of rich, dark soil. "How could I have forgotten? I must be as worried as my Nonna looks," he muttered.

"We will speak of this later, old man," Nonna stated crisply. "When we are alone and I do not disgrace you in front of—" She broke off, no doubt at a loss for how to describe them. Family? Friends? More likely, enemies.

"This is Gabriel," Primo hastened to introduce. "And his wife-to-be, Katerina Malloy."

Nonna inclined her snowy head in a gracious nod, all the while hostile, hazel eyes inspected them critically. There was a spark of anger there, along with something that wavered on the cusp of rejection. And yet, Kat also saw a stunning helplessness, a sorrow that deepened the lines of a face graced with the sort of bone structure that gave Nonna a beauty that would undoubtedly last until the day she died. She turned the full power of that look on Gabe and her mouth compressed, but not from anger, Kat suddenly realized. If anything Nonna attempted to keep her lips from trembling. As though to confirm it, tears welled into her eyes and slid silently down her cheeks.

It was too much for Gabe. He broke from Kat's side and dropped to one knee in front of his grandmother, gently taking her hands in his. "Don't," he murmured. "If my presence causes you this much pain, I'll leave. It was wrong of me to come here. To ask this favor of you."

"Hush, *nipote*." Nonna slipped her hands from his and

gathered his face, lifting it to hers. Then she kissed him. "Forgive a foolish old woman who believed that because my Dominic did wrong, what he created was wrong, as well. If I'd looked with my heart instead of my head, I'd have seen this, for I have always had the sight. I have always seen what others cannot or will not."

Gabe shut his eyes, fighting desperately to shore up his barriers. But it was a losing battle. They crumbled beneath her compassionate regard. "You need to know I despise him for what he did to my mother," he confessed. "My own father and—"

She shushed him again. "How could you feel anything else when you were not given the chance to know him as a son should know his father? But now you have found us. At long last you have come home to become one of us. A Dante."

He shook his head. "I'm not," he denied. "I'll never be a Dante."

She laughed, the sound like the warmth and cheer of Christmas holding at bay the cold rawness of a barren winter. "How illogical you are. How can you not be what you have always been?"

"I'm a Moretti," Gabe stated through gritted teeth. "And I am the most logical person you will ever meet."

She gave a dainty snort. "And these Morettis, they have welcomed you? They have provided for you what the Dantes have not?"

He didn't answer immediately, not until she pinched his cheek, making him feel all of five. "No," he admitted. "My mother's family disowned her when they discovered she was pregnant and unmarried."

"My poor boy." Tears welled in her eyes once again and a ferocity grew there, a blistering determination. "No matter. After all these years, we have found you, Gabriel. We will never disown what belongs to us."

He stiffened in open rejection. She'd touched on the one point he found most unforgiveable. "That's not true. You turned your back on us after Dominic died. You knew we existed, but you refused to acknowledge us. You may not have disowned us, but you did reject us."

Nonna shot an alarmed look at Primo. "Is this true? You have known about Gabriel since we lost our Dominic?"

"What is this? What is this?" He hastened to Gabe's side. "You think we have turned our back on you? Who told you such a lie?"

Gabe hesitated, unwilling to set a match to the turmoil that swirled across the surface of their conversation like a toxic slick of crude oil. He spared a swift look in Kat's direction, who offered a nod of encouragement. He understood the unspoken message. The time had come for total honesty. "He told us you knew. My...my father. That you wanted nothing to do with us."

It took a moment for his words to sink in. The instant they did, Nonna rocked back and forth, tears welling in her eyes and sliding down her lined cheeks. "Oh, Dominic. What have you done? Why did you keep this from us? Your son was an innocent. He needed his Nonna and Primo, and you never told us."

Unable to help himself, he took his grandmother in his arms and simply held her. Then he felt the strength of his grandfather's arms around them both. There was no longer any question about whether or not he *should* be one of them. He knew the truth in that moment. He *was* one of them.

Only one person remained on the outside. He turned to Kat, reached for her. She tried to evade his grasp and he understood why. She considered herself an outsider. But he wouldn't allow it. She needed family as much as he did. He overrode her incipient protest and drew her in. He couldn't quite explain it, didn't dare analyze it, but the instant her warmth and strength joined them, it felt right. The circle melded, became complete. They were bound in some inexplicable way, united in pain and loss, yet found. Accepted. Loved.

There was no awkwardness when they broke apart. Somehow his grandparents wouldn't allow it. "So," Primo said. "It is done. You are one of us."

Gabe spared his grandparents a sharp glance. "You really didn't know about me?"

"I only recently was made aware. Your cousin Gianna told me about running into you during her visit to Seattle, mentioned how much you look like Severo. We knew by then that Dominic had had an affair with your mother, but had only recently suspected that she might have become pregnant as a result. I began looking into it after Gianna found you."

"Family is everything to us," Nonna said with quiet simplicity. "We never would have turned from you if Dominic had told us of your existence."

Gabe heard the ring of truth in her voice and nodded. "Thank you."

Primo stood at Nonna's side, a united front. "I will have my car take you to see my assistant. Lucia has volunteered to be your wedding planner. She will help arrange for the marriage license. Then, while she takes your bride to pick out her wedding gown, Sev has agreed to meet you at Dantes Exclusive to select the wedding rings." He offered a tentative smile. "This is agreeable to you?"

"Sev's going to meet with me?" More than anything Gabe wanted to refuse. But he couldn't. Not when his grandmother watched him so anxiously. They were doing everything possible to reach out. The least he could do was meet them halfway, especially since he'd approached them. "Sure. Not a problem. We were bound to meet sometime."

"It will not be easy for either of you," Primo said. "But it is long past time the two of you know each other as brothers. Try to remember that he is an innocent in all of this, as well. And he feels Dominic's betrayal of his mother as keenly as you feel it for yours."

"There's one difference." Gabe took Kat's hand in his. For some reason, the touch of those warm, slender fingers offered him an unexpected solace, one he hadn't anticipated, but didn't hesitate to accept. "He grew up with the Dante name from the day he was born. I didn't."

Kat fell in love with Lucia the moment they met, amazed to discover Gabe's sister possessed a personality as different from Gabe's as her appearance. While her brother tended to keep his emotions on ice—except for the occasional volcanic explosions—Lucia's face revealed every thought and feeling, from the apprehension of their first meeting to the delight of discovering a kindred spirit. It all came through in each gesture and intonation.

What amused her the most was when Lucia and Gabe balled their hands into fists and linked index fingers before embracing. "It was our private signal to each other and to our mother," Lucia explained afterward. "Sort of an unwritten code to let the other know we're there for them and that we love them. That we have their backs."

Obtaining the marriage license didn't take any time at all, though it soon became clear that Primo had pulled a few strings in order to get them preferential treatment. The only awkward moment occurred when Gabe caught a glimpse of her application.

"That's your birth date?" he asked in an odd voice.

"Yes." She gave him a puzzled glance. "I'll be twenty-five in a couple months. Why?"

"You were only twenty when…?"

She appreciated that he didn't finish his question in front of a curious Lucia. "Technically I was nineteen. How old did you think I was?"

"Not nineteen." His mouth compressed. "I didn't realize Jessa was so much older than you."

Kat glanced at his information. "I've got news for you. She was older than both of us."

He immediately shook his head. "That can't be right. She told me—" He broke off. "Maybe we'll save this discussion for a later time."

"What's the point?" she asked quietly. "After all, it won't change anything."

For once, he didn't have an answer. When they were finished with the paperwork, they split up, Gabe heading for Dantes Exclusive, while Lucia took charge of their shopping expedition. Her natural exuberance had faded and Kat couldn't help but wonder if she'd finally realized who Gabe was marrying—or rather, what she'd been accused of five years ago.

Sure enough, she broached the subject, her tone unnaturally clipped. "You're Jessa's cousin, aren't you?"

"Yes." Kat didn't bother to expound. Offering any sort of explanation seemed futile. Lucia caught her bottom lip between her teeth, clearly debating whether or not to speak her mind, which would have been amusing under different circumstances. "You might as well go ahead and say it," she said kindly.

"Okay." Lucia snatched a quick breath and blurted, "I hated your cousin. I know I shouldn't speak ill of the dead, but I thought she was all wrong for Gabe. If she hadn't died in that car wreck, they'd have been divorced by now. I guarantee it."

"Uh—"

Kat didn't manage more than that small squeak before Lucia launched into speech again. "And she'd have taken my brother to the cleaners before she finished with him. Not that she'd have had to. He'd probably have given her anything she wanted just to get rid of her." She made a face. "Okay, maybe not anything. He would have done everything in his power to get his hands on Mom's necklace, assuming Jessa inherited it. Not that she would have let it go easily. Knowing her, she'd have used Heart's Desire to get *her* heart's desire which was every last penny Gabe possessed. Lord, I hope you're not like her." She turned a fierce glare on Kat. "Because if you are, I'm not holding back this time. I will find a way to take you down."

It took Kat a moment to process the flood of information, before admitting, "Gabe and I are marrying so he can have Heart's Desire and I can reconcile with my grandmother. The marriage is just temporary."

"Oh." Lucia's brow wrinkled. "Well, that's not going to work."

"Why?"

"Don't you know?" She tossed a grin in Kat's direction. "How can it be temporary when it's clear to anyone with half a brain you're crazy about each other?"

From that point on, Lucia and Kat became firm friends. It felt odd. It also felt good. She'd never had anyone treat her with such immediate and spontaneous affection. There'd always been barriers before, even during her time in Italy. Of course those barriers were of her own making. After the scandal, she'd been cautious to the extreme, afraid to open up to anyone in case they hurt her the way Jessa had. Somehow, Lucia had a way of sweeping past all that, as good at opening up others as she was at opening herself to them. And yet, Kat didn't have a moment's doubt that her secrets were safe with Lucia.

"We certainly have our work cut out for us," Lucia said, sweeping into the first bridal shop. She ticked off on her fingers. "There's the wedding gown, of course. The veil. The undergarments. Shoes. Something gorgeous and sexy for your wedding night. A few extra outfits to throw in just because."

"I don't need a few extra outfits."

Lucia shot an admiring glance at the dress Kat wore. "Probably not, but what the hell, right? And once we have your wedding gown picked out, I'll know what sort of flowers to order."

"I think I hear my credit card whimpering."

"Don't be ridiculous," Lucia protested. "The Dantes are paying for everything."

"Oh, no, they most certainly are not," Kat shot back. "I won't allow it. And I guarantee, Gabe won't, either."

Lucia frowned in genuine concern. "You can't refuse. You'll break Primo's heart if you do."

"I'm afraid he'll just have to live with a broken heart," she stated in her most implacable voice. "It'll mend."

Not that her tone cut any ice with Lucia. She swept aside Kat's comment as though it were inconsequential. "You don't understand. He won't be disappointed, he'll be offended. And if you offend Primo, you offend all of the Dantes." She shrugged. "It's an Italian thing. Offend one, offend all."

Damn. After five years in Italy, she should have anticipated that. "Gabe will not be happy."

"Gabe will have to learn to live with his unhappiness, especially considering where he's going right now," Lucia said tartly. "His meeting with Sev won't be easy. My half brother has issues when it comes to my mother, and with Gabe in particular."

"Why Gabe in particular?"

Lucia hesitated and a profound sadness crept into her expression. "I suppose it would be with both of us if he knew I existed." She pretended to give her full attention to the designer gowns on display.

"Lucia?" Kat prompted gently.

"I think it's because of The Inferno," she confessed softly.

"You've lost me."

She spared Kat a swift look over her shoulder. Her eyes darkened, the teal-blue reflecting endless pain. "If Cara Moretti was Dominic's Inferno soul mate…"

It only took Kat a moment to connect the dots. When she reached the logical conclusion, she winced. "What does that make Sev's mother?"

"Exactly. *Not* Dominic's Inferno soul mate. That's why I can never have any sort of meaningful relationship with my half brothers. The fact that Dominic never truly loved their mother would always stand between us."

Primo's car dropped Gabe near the Embarcadero, in the heart of the financial district. He'd been directed to a smoked glass door etched with the initials DE, and used the call button nearby to announce himself. A buzzer immediately sounded, releasing the door lock and allowing him access to Dantes Exclusive.

While the outside appeared unassuming, the interior was anything but. An understated opulence permeated the reception area, echoed by a staff member dressed in an elegant suit and tie. He gave a start of surprise, bordering on shock at Gabe's appearance, no doubt due to his close resemblance to Sev. Then he offered a polite greeting and escorted Gabe to a private elevator that went directly to the penthouse level.

Clearly, he'd been expected. He stepped off the car into a massive room that could have been mistaken for a private residence. His shoes vanished into the thick, dove-gray carpeting that gave the area a lavish, yet intimate feel, echoing what he'd experienced at Dantes corporate office building.

The employee gestured toward a glittering wet bar at one end of the room. "Would you care for a drink?"

He might just kill for one, Gabe decided. "No, thanks." He'd also be damned before he accepted anything else from the Dantes.

"Mr. Dante will be right with you," his escort said—warned?—before stepping back into the elevator and leaving him alone in the room.

Gabe wandered deeper into luxury where plants and elaborate fresh flower arrangements gave the area an added warmth. Divans covered in gray and white pinstripes dotted the room, along with silk chairs in a rich ruby-red, all with glass tables placed in front of the sitting areas. The tables were a bit higher than normal coffee tables, with overhead spots throwing circles of blazing light on each table, leaving the chairs and couches in soft shadow. No doubt the tables had been specifically designed to showcase Dantes' fabulous gems for some of the company's more exclusive clientele.

A door opposite him opened and a man entered the room. Gabe didn't have a single doubt this was Sev Dante. Based on Gianna's reaction when she and Gabe first met, as well as the DE employee just now, he'd been anticipating the resemblance, assuming they would look quite a bit alike. But he didn't expect to meet someone who could have passed for his twin. Sev spared him a single shocked glare, then paused by a wet bar, splashing amber liquor into two glasses. He approached and offered one of the drinks.

"If you're experiencing anything close to what I am, I'm betting you need this as badly as I do," Sev said.

"Hell, yes," Gabe answered, accepting the tumbler.

They both took a swift swallow, then continued to eye one another with undisguised dislike. "So, who goes first?" Sev asked. The question held the unmistakable slap of a challenge.

Gabe didn't hesitate in snatching up the gauntlet. "I will. Just so you know, if I had any other choice, I'd have been just as happy never meeting any of you. I don't want anything from you. Ever."

"And yet, here you are, expecting us to acknowledge you," Sev shot back. "In my book, that's wanting something."

Gabe's mouth tightened. "Okay, fine. I want something."

"And just so you know, if Primo hadn't insisted on my being here, I'd have been just as happy never meeting you, too." Sev bared his teeth in a rough semblance of a smile. "I can also categorically state—just so we're crystal clear on the subject—that not only don't I want anything from you, I wouldn't accept anything from you if I were on my deathbed and you possessed my only hope for salvation."

Gabe thrust his nose toward one identical to his own. "See, there's where we differ. I *would* accept what you possessed. I'd just make damn sure I found a way to make you suffer for your generosity."

Sev's nose thrust out another inch, as did his chin. "Excellent idea. Since you're the one who needs what I have, let's see if I can't make you suffer before I give it to you."

They both hesitated. Gabe broke the confused silence. "Okay, I gotta admit," he said. "I don't understand a word of what we just said."

"Neither did I," Sev concurred. "But I think what we both mean is that we despise each other and would be only too happy to make life as miserable as possible for the other person. Does that sum it up?"

Ah, good. A negotiation. The familiar territory put him on sound footing and also made him realize just how off-balance he'd been this entire time. "I think we have the bare bones laid out. And I have some suggestions where we can take it from there."

"You want another drink while we put some flesh on those bones?"

"Only if we stop speaking in metaphors."

"Thank God."

Sev added a couple fingers to each glass and eyed Gabe over the rim. "Considering how happy we all were not having to deal with each other's existence, why step forward now? What's changed?"

Gabe rubbed his thumb across his palm. "If it weren't for this damn Inferno, I wouldn't be here. But I don't have any choice, not if I want to protect Kat."

"Your bride-to-be?" At Gabe's nod, unholy amusement glittered in eyes identical to Gabe's. "You two experienced The Inferno when you first touched?"

"Yes."

"And how will it help to have the Dantes acknowledge the connection—"

"For want of a better word," Gabe inserted smoothly.

Sev growled. "You'd prefer a different word? Fine. How about *bastard*? There. Is that a better word?"

Gabe shrugged. He'd heard the word used in reference to him so often, it no longer had the power to wound when someone attempted to use it like a weapon. He'd learned to deal with what he was years ago. To accept his illegitimacy in a way his mother and sister never had. "Do you think calling me a bastard changes anything? That I'm offended? Hurt?" He gave a harsh laugh. "I've got news for you, Sev. I *am* a bastard. And do you know why? It's because that's what our father made me."

"You think I don't know that?" Sev shot right back. "Not a day goes by that I'm not aware of your existence and the implications of that existence."

"Oh, man, I feel for you." Sarcasm ran roughshod over Gabe's response. "Poor you. Having to deal with the fact that you've got a bastard brother. Try living it. Then come crying to me."

"Hell, hotshot. You're the one standing square on Dante property, hat in hand. If anyone's crying…"

Gabe saw red. He acted without thought. Spinning around, he heaved his glass at the nearest wall. It exploded with a high-pitched crystalline shriek, and splattered shards of glass and amber liquid across the pristine wall and floor beneath. The Scotch bled downward, as though weeping bitter tears. He gulped air, stunned by his utter lack of control. He struggled against the white-hot fury whipping through him, shoving him closer to the edge than he could ever remember being shoved, knowing the least wrong word would push him into the seething abyss.

He swung around to face Sev. "I'm not here for myself, you ass. I want nothing from you. I'm here for Kat. To protect her. As far as I'm concerned, you can take the Dante name and shove it."

"Jealous?"

Eight

That single taunting word stripped through years of denial. Laid Gabe bare. How had Sev done it? It took all of two minutes in the same room together before he'd nailed Gabe's one weakness and broken through the iceman façade to what seethed beneath. To what he'd fought so hard to suppress…and failed.

And he'd hit on the single key vulnerability Gabe had spent his entire life attempting to deny. Taking a deep breath, he forced himself to open that locked door and stare at what he'd hidden inside. To confront the truth from an adult's perspective and deal with what a child had buried so many years before, desperate to conceal that truth from anyone and everyone. He stiffened his spine and met Sev's gaze squarely, allowing the ugliness free rein. After all, what did it matter what this man thought of him, so long as he protected Kat? After what he'd done five years ago, he owed her at least that much.

"Yes. Yes, I am jealous." he whispered. The gut-wrenching pain slipped free of his iron grip and he released it, unable to contain it for another second. "You have what my mother and sister would have given anything to possess. You've lived a life we'll never know. Do you blame me for wanting to turn my back on what was denied me? For despising the man who created us, then deserted us?"

"Sister?" Sev demanded in shock. "You have a *sister?*"

Damn, damn, *damn*. That's what happened when he lost control. "A twin," he reluctantly admitted.

"Does Primo know?"

"No. Not yet, and I prefer to keep it that way until she's ready to tell him, herself."

"Is she… Is she—" Sev broke off and shook his head.

Was that concern Gabe heard? It sounded almost protective, which struck him as utterly ridiculous. Why would Sev feel the least bit protective toward Lucia? Unless… Unless they were more alike than he cared to admit. It was an unsettling thought. "Is she…what?" he asked suspiciously.

"I want to say, is she okay. But how can she be?" Sev sighed. "How can any of us be okay with any part of this?"

"She wasn't okay for a very long time," Gabe found himself admitting. "But she's…coping."

Sev fell silent. "I found out about Dad's affair right after his death. There were letters." He grimaced. "I didn't know until recently that the affair had resulted in children."

"And if you had known?"

He didn't hesitate. "I'd have told Primo right away. He and Nonna brought us to live with them after our parents died. Of course, I was in college by then, but my brothers…" A hint of a smile drifted across his mouth. "Knowing Primo, he'd have taken you and your sister in, too. Raised us as a family. Knocked our heads together until we learned to accept each other."

Gabe returned the smile, amazed by how natural it felt. "From what little I know about our grandfather, I suspect you're right."

The muscles ridging Sev's jaw tightened. "Dad loved her, you know. Your mother. Our father loved her in a way he never loved my mother." The confession came hard, almost as hard as Gabe's admitting he'd been jealous of Sev and his brothers. "Maybe you can understand it a little better now that you've experienced The Inferno. My brothers and I, we were the product of his marriage. But we were never the product of his heart."

Gabe swore beneath his breath. "Still, you bear his name."

"True. But you and your sister and mother owned his heart." His mouth tightened and bitter grief darkened eyes identical to Gabe's. "So it would seem we both are jealous of something the other possesses."

It was a bizarre thought, one that twisted how Gabe saw himself and his family and the Dantes. "So, what now?"

"Maybe now we simply accept what can't be changed and move on. Maybe figure out what we can change in the future." Sev allowed that to sink in before deliberately switching the subject. "Tell me how our name will protect your bride-to-be. Kat, is it?"

"I need the Dantes to acknowledge the connection so she won't be vilified in the press."

Sev frowned. "Why would they do that?"

"She was unjustly accused of having an affair with her cousin's fiancé. Benson Winters? He was a senatorial candidate at the time." Sev nodded his recognition of the name and Gabe continued. "She was found in bed with him."

Sev's expression closed down. "She was caught in bed with him, but she's innocent." He paused a beat. "You're sure?"

He spoke in a noncommittal tone, but Gabe could hear

the doubt leaching through the words. "It's a little hard to have an affair with a man when you've never slept with anyone before," he retorted.

To his surprise, Sev stepped right over the line from doubt to immediate acceptance. "Well, who was the son of a bitch who accused her? And why the hell would he do something like that?" Anger stirred in his gaze with the sort of protective rage Gabe found all too familiar. It disconcerted him to discover one more similarity between them. "And why the hell haven't you beaten the living snot out of him?"

"Because I'm the son of a bitch who accused her."

"You." Sev's eyes narrowed and Gabe suspected he teetered on the edge of personally administering the beating he'd recommended. Apparently that protective streak came from the Dante side of the family. Who knew? "Why? Why would you do that?"

"Because I found her in his bed. I don't have all the facts about what happened. Yet," he added. "And obviously, there's more to the story than my attempting to right a wrong. There are reasons—reasons I'd rather not go into—for our needing everyone to accept our marriage and believe it's genuine."

"Which I assume it is." Sev tossed back the last of his drink. "At least, it is if you two have been hit with The Inferno."

Gabe didn't bother to correct him. The Dantes would discover the truth on that score as soon as he and Kat divorced. But maybe he could obtain a more realistic explanation for The Inferno before that happened. "As long as you brought up the subject…"

Sev laughed. "You have questions about The Inferno."

"I asked Primo, but—"

"Our grandfather has strong opinions on the subject."

"I gather you don't agree with those opinions?" It came

as a relief to discover Sev didn't buy into the fairy tale. "So, you're just humoring him?"

"You want me to say that The Inferno will go away. That it's not real."

"It isn't real."

Sev laughed in genuine amusement. "That's what I thought until it hit me the first time Francesca and I touched. That's what my brothers all thought until it happened to them. Just as it happened to all four of our cousins. Almost all of us fought it. And every one of us lost the battle. Face it. If you're a Dante, you're stuck with The Inferno."

"I'm not a Dante!"

Sev shook his head in disgust. "That's what I planned to tell you. In fact, I'd intended to make it clear with my fists, if necessary." He shrugged philosophically. "Looks like we're both wrong. You're a Dante whether you want to be or not. Hell, whether *we* want you to be or not."

"Look, it doesn't matter what you call me. Not really. Once Kat and I are married, we'll be out of all your lives," Gabe insisted.

"Sorry, but it won't be that simple," Sev warned. "You're not a Dante one minute and then not one the next. It's all or nothing. Primo and Nonna won't allow it to go down any other way. As much as I hate to admit it—" He stuck out his hand. "Looks like we're brothers."

Gabe stared at the hand Sev offered for an endless moment. Instinct warned that if he accepted it, everything would change. His life would never be the same again. He'd become a different person. He'd be accepting something he'd spent his entire life denying. Granted, it was his choice. But once the decision had been made, it couldn't be undone.

He looked into Sev's eyes and saw himself. Saw the same tawny eyes which had been passed from father to son through the generations. Saw the same passion and fierce determination. The same protectiveness. Saw features cut into harsh lines by a life fully lived, filled with both happiness and pain. Saw himself, the good as well as the bad.

He stared again at the hand being offered. Accepting it would forever alter him, take him from being a Moretti…to becoming a Dante. And he knew which he wanted, which he'd always wanted, if he'd been honest with himself.

Without any further hesitation, he took his brother's hand.

Kat woke on her wedding day to a fierce wind and a leaden sky unleashing a torrent of rain. She stood at the window of the suite Primo insisted on booking at Le Premier, a five-star hotel on Nob Hill, and struggled against disappointment. The rain made her think of tears. And though she claimed to never, ever cry—despite a single aberration the first time Gabe made love to her—she couldn't deny feeling a tiny bit tearful when she stared out at the gray, wet curtain blanketing San Francisco.

Her grandmother joined her at the window. "It rained on my wedding day, too."

"Did it bring you bad luck?"

Matilda laughed, and for the first time in more than five years it came with a familiar ease. For some reason the sound had those tears Kat held at bay welling into her eyes. "Not even a little. Your grandfather and I looked like two drowned rats when it was all said and done. But it led… Well, it led to a very special wedding night."

Kat bowed her head. "Gam, I'm sorry. I'm so sorry I hurt you."

"Hush now, child. It's not you who should apologize, but me. You wrote to me the entire time you were gone, kept in touch while I allowed pride to get in my way. Allowed moral outrage to hold me apart from you for five lonely years instead of following my heart and accepting that you were young and foolish and made a dreadful mistake. Forgive me if it takes a little time for me to be the grandmother you deserve." She gathered Kat close. "But no matter what, always remember that I love you, Katerina."

"I love you, too, Gam." She burrowed against the woman who'd been mother, grandmother and confidante, and inhaled the familiar scent of her, a powdery fragrance lightly accented with rose. It was like coming home, even if everything had changed. Even if she couldn't quite regain the relationship they'd once shared. "I don't want to lose you. Not after I just found you again."

"There's still time." She gave Kat a final hug. "I brought Heart's Desire with me. I thought maybe you'd like to wear it today."

Kat pulled back and smiled in delight. "I'd love to wear it. It would mean the world to Gabe."

Matilda crossed the room and removed a velvet box from her purse. She gripped it tightly, hesitation disturbing the even tenor of her expression. "This marriage…it's all happened so fast. You…you do love Gabe? That is the reason you're marrying?"

Oh, dear. She didn't want to lie to her grandmother. But she couldn't admit the entire truth. She didn't dare. "I realize it's fast. But Gabe explained to you about his connection to the Dantes, right? And he explained about The Inferno, what it is and—" For some reason she couldn't prevent a blush. "And how it works?"

A small smile touched Matilda's mouth. "I have to admit, I find it terribly romantic. Not that I consider myself the romantic sort. But to feel that sort of love from the first moment you touch… And best of all it was with Gabe. I adore him, you know. I always have."

Kat approached her grandmother and offered her most reassuring smile. "Then you can trust him to do what's right."

Matilda released her breath in a sigh, clearly relieved. "Yes, yes. Of course." Fortunately, she didn't pick up on the fact that her original question had never been answered. She handed Kat the box. "I have to admit I haven't seen the necklace in quite some time. If I'd known the wedding would happen so soon, I'd have had it cleaned for you."

Kat carried it to a small table covered in a linen runner and shifted a lamp closer so it spotlighted the center section. Then she spread the necklace beneath the high-powered light. The diamonds burst into flames.

"It really is spectacular," she murmured, then frowned, leaning in.

Something wasn't quite right. She studied the necklace more carefully and realized that not all of the stones contained the same flash and glitter she would have expected from fire diamonds, or that she remembered it having five years ago. Her frown deepened. Was it possible that they weren't all fire diamonds? She peered closer, wishing she had a loupe. Were they even real diamonds? Could the original design have combined regular stones with those unearthed in the Dante mines? Her stomach clenched. It was possible, wasn't it?

Possible, maybe, but highly improbable.

One way or another, she needed to find out and fast. Until she uncovered the truth, she didn't dare wear the necklace, not in front of countless Dantes, all of whom could spot a fake a mile away. And what about her marriage to Gabe? If the necklace was a fake—or missing a significant number of the original diamonds—would he still be so quick to marry her? Or would he wait in order to verify the necklace appraised…and determine whether or not she was pregnant?

Okay, okay. Stay calm. It was an old necklace. It was entirely possible that thirty or more years ago the Dantes didn't use fire diamonds, exclusively. Francesca! Francesca would know. Kat would simply solicit the opinion of Sev's wife. As their top designer, she'd be able to determine the authenticity of both the necklace and the stones. Until then…

She glanced at her grandmother and forced out a smile. "You know, it occurs to me that if I wear this necklace the Dantes might recognize the piece, as well as its significance. It might not be the most diplomatic decision to wear jewelry Dominic gave to someone other than his wife, even if she was Gabe's mother. I wouldn't want to risk damaging his relationship with his family now that they're on the verge of a reconciliation."

Matilda frowned. "I hadn't considered that." She gave it a moment's thought. "Perhaps you could give it to him tonight as a wedding gift?"

"I think that's an excellent idea," Kat replied, relieved beyond measure. "Or possibly as a Christmas gift. What do you think?"

"I think he'd appreciate that, as well. If you wait until Christmas, you'd have time to get it cleaned," Matilda pointed out.

An old-fashioned doorbell rang, putting an end to their discussion, and Kat quickly stowed the necklace in the suite safe while Matilda went to open the door. Lucia entered in her role as wedding planner, the female half of the Dante contingent in tow, there to assist with the pre-wedding preparations. To Kat's frustration, Francesca wasn't one of them, having agreed to cover babysitting duties in order to free up the others.

It was interesting to discover that Gabe's sister possessed his same attention to detail, along with his ability to manage and direct. In no time, she had everyone scurrying to tackle all the endless tasks necessary to get a lot accomplished in a very short period of time. Kat debated whether or not to escape the organized chaos in search of Gabe and warn him of her suspicions about the necklace. But Lucia put a swift end to that possibility when asked, oh so casually, about his whereabouts.

"He's not here, and don't even bother asking where he is. None of us will tell you."

"Well, of course not," Gianna added with a mischievous grin. "You can't see the groom before the ceremony. It's bad luck."

The women all burst out laughing, one of them explaining, "Gia had a confession to make to her husband, Constantine, one that couldn't wait until after the ceremony. So she invaded the groom's room, despite risking very bad luck. It's become a family joke."

"I promise I won't invade Gabe's room before we're married," Kat began, "but—"

"You can't call him, either. Primo took away his cell phone. I think he's probably the only one who could have gotten Gabe to cough it up, too," Lucia whispered with a grin. "I wish I could have seen that."

So, that cut off her only other avenue of contact. Kat spared a glance toward the windows. "Seems like the weather really has brought bad luck."

"Rain is not bad luck," Nonna insisted. "*È buona fortuna.* It brings you good luck. It cleanses all the bad from your past. Rain is also a sign of fertility. Babies. It brings you the baby."

"Is she going to have boys or girls?" Gianna asked. She winked at Kat. "My grandmother has the eye. She hasn't gotten a single one wrong, yet. So, which is it, Nonna? Boys or girls?"

"Yes," Nonna said placidly.

The women all laughed. "There you have it," Gianna's mother, Elia said. "You're either going to have a boy or a girl."

The women turned their attention to laying out her gown and veil, and setting up stations for makeup and hair. On the far side of the room, Gianna and Matilda had their heads together. Based on the snatch of conversation that accompanied their laughter, they were comparing wedding day stories.

Nonna beckoned to Kat, waiting to speak until she'd come close enough not to be overheard. "You wish to know what you will have?"

Kat shrugged. Why not? "Sure."

Nonna touched just beneath the knotted sash holding Kat's robe closed. A hint of color touched her cheeks. "I did not wish to say in front of the others since you and Gabriel should not have made this baby before saying your vows." She gave a shrug of resignation. "But what is done is done. Soon you will be married and your son protected from the life Gabriel experienced."

Kat choked. "I'm…I'm pregnant?" Her voice rose in a breathless squeak and she sank to her knees beside Nonna's chair. "You mean, *now?*"

Gabe's grandmother chuckled. "This is usually what pregnant means. You are not far along. The spark is so very tiny, I almost missed it. Just the barest of flickers. But strong. Stubborn. A fighter."

"A son." She grappled with the concept. "You said it will be a boy."

"This first one, yes. The two that follow will be girls. Twins. With pretty reddish hair like yours, but with their father's golden eyes. Your son, he will have your eye color." Nonna smiled. "I see you do not believe me."

"I—" Kat shook her head. "I don't know what to believe."

"I am not offended. In time you will see I am right and then you will not question." She frowned. "You are upset. Does this not make you happy?"

Kat bowed her head. "It makes me very happy," she whispered. "But I'm not sure whether it will make Gabe happy."

Nonna appeared astounded at the suggestion. "Why would Gabriel not be happy?"

"Because it means he'll be stuck with me."

"Stuck with…?" She shook her head and called to her daughter-in-law. "Elia, *che cosa significa* 'stuck with me,' eh?"

"*Intrappolati.*"

Nonna turned a sharp gaze on Kat. "You and Gabriel, you have experienced The Inferno, yes?" At Kat's nod, she smiled in relief. "Do not worry about this stickiness. The Inferno, it will unstick you."

"You mean, it goes away?"

Nonna laughed. "No, no. It never goes away. You just do not feel sticky. You only feel love. It is like *il bambino.* It must have time to become. You marry Gabriel and you will have all the years God blesses you with to become. *Capito?*"

Oh, Kat understood, all right. She just wasn't sure she believed. But the plans Gabe had set in motion were moving too fast to stop. Her hand slid low on her abdomen, settling over the baby Nonna claimed rested there. If she really were pregnant, she couldn't stop the marriage, even if she tried. Even if Heart's Desire was a fake. If Gabe so much as suspected she carried his baby, he wouldn't rest until he'd placed his ring on her finger in order to make absolutely certain his child didn't experience the stigma he had growing up. Still, she hated the idea of tying him to a marriage he thought temporary.

And yet, throughout the rest of the morning she caught herself cradling the spark of new life she and Gabe may have created.

A baby.

* * *

The wedding was everything Kat could have wanted, and then some.

She wore a gown that she and Lucia had fallen in love with the second they'd seen it, a delicious blend of elegance and romance. The women helped hook her into the lacey, fitted bodice, exclaiming that it made her waist appear miniscule. They smoothed the skirt of the gown around her, one that flared out in a wide bell with a dramatic chapel length train. To her stunned delight, Nonna provided an antique tiara, studded with fire diamonds, clearly from Dantes personal collection. The tulle veil attached to the tiara and swept to the floor, framing her in softness, the scalloped edges trimmed with lace that matched her gown.

There'd been heated debate among the women over her hair, but she'd held firm, quietly insisting that she wear it down. It was how Gabe preferred it and as soon as she explained that, they swiftly shifted gears, discussing the exact style that would suit both the veil and her facial structure. In the end, they pulled the sides back and up and curled the rest, allowing it to tumble down her back and shoulders. Then they wove a narrow silver beaded ribbon through the strands, anchored with bits of mistletoe and holly, a reminder that Christmas was right around the corner, only ten days away.

By the time they left for the chapel, the rain had subsided and the sun beamed through a series of large, puffy clouds. The ride from the hotel took no time and the women assisted Kat with her gown so it wouldn't get damp during the climb to the stone chapel topping the hill. They left her in the garden on one side to await the start of the ceremony, while assisting Matilda to her seat in the chapel. Kat stared out at the glorious view of the bay and its islands, along with the distinctive red arches of the Golden Gate Bridge, struggling to remain calm and focused while nerves tried to get the better of her.

Maybe if she hadn't realized the necklace might be a fake… She glanced toward the chapel wondering if she could sneak in and speak to Gabe before the ceremony. Tell him about the necklace and give him the option of changing his mind. Before she could follow through on the thought, Primo joined her, looking dapper in his tux, puffing on his signature cigar.

She spared the chapel a final look of regret before turning her attention to Gabe's grandfather. "Thank you for offering to walk me down the aisle," she said.

"It is my pleasure. You look…" He shook his head, emotion welling into his eyes. "You look the way a bride should on her wedding day. Radiant, yes?"

She could feel her smile tremble at the edges, bordering on the tears she refused to let fall. "Thank you."

He took her hand in his. "You are nervous. It is understandable, but there is no need. You will discover this for yourself in the fullness of time." He gave her hand a fatherly squeeze. "Whether you realize it or not, you both love each other."

Kat instantly shook her head. "No, not after such a short time. It's not possible."

"It is fear that keeps you from admitting the truth. Gabriel is afraid you will betray him the way his father betrayed his mother, choosing to marry for financial gain instead of following his heart. Then when Dominic never returned to claim the child he had created out of wedlock, Gabe lost all ability to trust. It is why he continues to hold himself from his Primo and Nonna. But, you…" He hesitated, then shrugged. "I see your fear, but do not know you well enough to guess the cause."

"I'm afraid to trust, as well," she confessed. "I've also been betrayed in the past."

"You are afraid Gabriel will betray you?" Clearly, the thought astounded him.

She instinctively shook his head. "He just wants to protect me."

"Ah." Primo regarded her with a wealth of tenderness and wisdom in his antique gold eyes. "And you do not want him to confuse protectiveness for love."

"Yes." He'd summed it up in a nutshell.

"Gabriel is a Dante. He will always feel driven to protect those he loves. It is part of the fabric of who he is." Primo leaned forward and kissed her forehead. "So if he protects you, it is because he loves you."

Kat wished she could believe him. Considering Gabe had done everything in his power to protect Jessa, including destroy the woman he now intended to marry, she had her doubts. Despite what his grandfather claimed, he couldn't love her, not after so short a time. Therefore, he wasn't attempting to protect her out of love, but due to some other misguided notion. Maybe he was only marrying her out of guilt, to right a wrong. She flinched from the thought.

The chapel bells sounded, a joyful pealing that heralded the start of the ceremony. Primo gently covered her face with the veil and offered her arm, escorting her to a vestibule where Christmas scented the air. It had been decorated in a mix of snowy white ranunculus and red roses, poinsettias and garlands of cedar boughs. Someone handed her a cascading bouquet that mirrored the Yuletide decorations surrounding her, tied together with a silver beaded ribbon that matched the one wound through her hair. Lucia, maybe? Then, the bells faded on the crisp winter air, the sweet sound of a string quartet replacing them, joyfully announcing the arrival of the bride.

For a split second, panic set in and Kat couldn't move. What was she doing? Had she lost her mind? She'd only known this man a few short weeks. How could she contemplate marrying someone after mere days of acquaintance, despite what happened whenever they touched? It was wrong. It went against everything this ceremony stood for.

It was bad enough that she'd fallen into bed with Gabe, had surrendered herself heart, body and soul whenever he took her into his arms. But to compound the mistake by marrying him, especially when he believed it would give him his Heart's Desire? She couldn't do it.

She'd figure some other way to reconcile with her grandmother. They were halfway reconciled already, weren't they? As for Heart's Desire, she'd simply insist her grandmother give it to him, especially if it proved to be a fake or missing a significant portion of the original diamonds. She didn't need or want it. And the possibility of her pregnancy? How would she handle that? She closed her eyes, fighting to breathe. Why, oh why, had she chosen a fitted bodice when any second now it would squeeze the very breath from her lungs?

Primo urged her forward and she teetered at the threshold of the chapel, on the verge of bolting. The aisle stretched in front of her, an endless flow of snowy white, accented with bright red rose petals that led straight to Gabe. She stared at him, knowing that all he had to do was look at her with those demanding tawny eyes and she'd pull a Cinderella.

He stood ramrod straight, at an angle to her. Then, almost as though he sensed her desperation, he turned his head and their gazes collided. She could never explain what happened then. With every instinct she possessed clamoring that she run, a tiny tendril of emotion pushed its way upward from deep inside. Despite being so small and new, it held her immobile, forcing her to look, really look at Gabe. So, she did.

She witnessed a similar dawning in his expression, a

look of stunned disbelief, as though he'd never truly seen her before. Where before his gaze carried a hint of tarnished resolution, now it changed. It was as though the sun rose in his eyes, bright and golden and filled with warmth that invaded every part of her. She saw a bottomless well of desire. Not the hunger they'd shared the night they made love. But something more reverent, something that made her palm itch and pulsate.

Then he slowly raised his hand against the dark palette of his tux and formed a tight fist, his index finger lifting free to curve into a hook. It was almost as though she heard him say the words: *I have your back. I'm here for you. I'll protect you.* That one simple gesture snagged hold of her, linked her to him. Every bit of tension drained away and she moved toward him without hesitation. Her heart filled with hope, and something else. Something she couldn't quite identify.

And when he took her hand in his, index fingers linked, that small, persistent tendril blossomed. Became. She recognized it then. Her fear faded and she took a chance, opening herself to it, allowing it to fill her, deep and powerful, until it became a permanent part of the very warp and weft of her being.

Love.

She realized in that moment she loved Gabe Moretti and knew with an unwavering certainty she would love him for the rest of her life.

Nine

The endless round of photographs left Kat teetering on the edge of a total meltdown. Who knew? Who knew that she'd handle the ceremony with aplomb—with the exception of that one teeny, tiny panic attack beforehand. She also breezed through meeting an endless kaleidoscope of Dantes, even managing to match names to faces. Of course, it helped that she quickly picked up on their unique characteristics and created private nicknames for each.

There was Gabe 2 (Sev). Silver Tongue (Marco). Spock (Lazz). Rambo (Nicolò). Then came the cousins. The Protector (Luc). The Wolf (Rafe). The Dragon (Draco). Okay, that was a bit obvious, but it fit. And finally, The Princess (Gianna), who possessed all the best qualities of Kat's personal nickname for her and none of the less admirable traits. She had a slightly more difficult time remembering the wives' names, with the notable exception of Francesca. But then,

Francesca was also a jewelry designer, someone Kat hoped to one day work with.

Kat managed it all with aplomb. But the photographer utterly defeated her, driving her to the brink of insanity, first at the chapel, and then at Le Premier, during the reception hosted by the hotel. Finally, Gabe stepped in and, with a few terse words, arranged for a brief interlude of privacy. He guided Kat to an elegant divan off in one corner, and circled behind her. Leaning in, he massaged her shoulders.

"I think I'm going to melt," she murmured, her eyes drifting closed.

"You're doing fantastic. Better than I would have in your shoes."

She chuckled, sticking out a foot, the four-inch spikes glittering like fairy dust. "You couldn't wear my shoes. No man could."

"Considering the height of those heels, they'd be tough to run in. When you walked into the chapel and realized what you'd gotten yourself into, I thought you'd give it a try."

She winced. "You noticed?"

"I took one look at you and realized I should have posted guards at the door." He leaned in to whisper, "Of course, if you'd bolted, I'd have been about three seconds behind you."

She tilted her head back to smile up at him. "I doubt you'd have gotten far. I think the Dantes would have tackled you."

"Tackled me and beat the living crap out of me." She caught a hint of reluctant humor lurking behind the words. "And enjoyed every minute of it, too."

"Boys will be boys," she said lightly.

He circled around to sit beside her. "Just remember, once they'd finished with me, they'd have gone after you."

She laughed. "Probably to congratulate me for my good taste in dumping you."

Unable to help herself, she reached for him, desperate

for the reassurance of his touch. The instant their hands met, heat flared. Gabe bent to kiss her. And then Kat's eyes closed and she surrendered to the embrace, allowed it to overcome logic and common sense. To sink inside of her and nourish that tendril that had blossomed during their wedding ceremony.

A whir and flash interrupted them and Gabe tensed. He lifted his head and shot a single glare at the photographer, who scurried off. "I'd go after him, but I have a feeling I'm going to want a print of that one."

A keepsake of their temporary marriage? Hope filled her. Maybe it would turn into more than a temporary marriage. Maybe, given time, he'd discover what she had. That, despite the short time she'd known him and despite all that continued to stand between them, she'd fallen in love with him, knew to the depths of her being that he was the one. The only. Her soul mate.

Gabe leaned in. "I have something for you." He'd lowered his voice to an intimate level that shut out everyone and everything else. "I was going to give it to you during the ceremony, but decided to wait until tonight. But somehow this seems like the right time."

Something soft and feminine stirred within. "What is it?" she couldn't resist asking.

"It's an engagement ring." He reached into an inner pocket of his tux and removed a black velvet ring box with the distinctive DE logo imprinted on the outside. He gave a soft laugh. "I should have given it to you before we married. But, like everything else in our relationship, we've gotten this backward, too."

He flipped open the lid and removed the ring. Taking her hand in his, he slid it onto her finger where it nestled against her wedding band. Kat's breath caught. It was a stunning piece, clearly one of Francesca's designs. An impressive cushion-cut fire diamond topped the platinum filigree, accented on either side with a swirl of smaller fire diamonds that contained an almost pink cast, lending a fiery color to the flames that made the Dante diamonds unique in the world.

"Oh, Gabe." Her breath escaped in a rush. "It's stunning."

"It's part of Dantes' Eternity line." An odd quality crept through his voice. "They're all named, which I didn't realize when I chose it. Sev's wife, Francesca, designed all of the pieces for the line."

"Yes, I can tell." It also looked somewhat familiar. And then it hit her, caused a cascade of disparate emotions to flood her, longing and guilt, hope and shame. She moistened her lips, driven to say, "You know, in some ways it reminds me of Heart's Desire."

He hesitated for a fraction of a second. "There's a reason for that. Sev told me Francesca based the design on photos she'd seen of Heart's Desire."

She dared to look at him, saw something that went beyond mere passion stirring in his Dante eyes. "What's it called?"

"My Heart's Desire."

He's surprised her. "So similar? Is that why you chose it?"

He shook his head. "I chose the ring before Sev told me the name. Bizarre coincidence, don't you think?"

She had to tell him the truth. Now. Granted, it wouldn't change the fact that she went through with the marriage instead of giving him the option of cancelling it. But at least they could start their marriage off with all the cards on the table. "Gabe…"

Before she could say another word, Francesca approached. She bent to kiss Kat, offering Gabe an apologetic smile. "You look so happy off to yourselves I hate to interrupt. But, Primo wanted to speak to you privately. I'd be happy to keep Kat company in the meantime. We can talk

about jewelry design." Her chocolate brown eyes gleamed
with amusement. "I find it intriguing that your mother was
a jewelry designer and that you're also married to one. It has
such a nice symmetry to it, don't you think?"

Gabe's hand slipped from Kat's shoulder just as the opportunity to confess all slipped away. "That it does." He
stood. "If you'll excuse me, I'll go see what Primo wants."

Kat waited until he was out of earshot before speaking.
"Actually, I was hoping to discuss something with you before we returned to Seattle. I wondered if you'd give me
your opinion."

Francesca perked up. "Is it jewelry related?"

Kat nodded. "It's about Heart's Desire. I'd like you to
look at the necklace."

"You have it with you?" Excitement blossomed in her
expression at Kat's nod. "I'd kill to see an example of Cara
Moretti's work. We have photos of her designs, but none of
the actual pieces."

"Would you be willing to take a quick look now? It's in
the safe in my suite." She spared Gabe a glance, concerned
to see he looked even grimmer than when he'd left them.
Whatever Primo was saying, it clearly packed an emotional
punch. "We probably have time to run upstairs before we're
scheduled to cut the cake."

The two slipped from the ballroom and took the elevator to the suite. Someone had cleaned the rooms in the few
hours since she'd last been here. All the feminine clutter
and chaos had disappeared, replaced by flowers, chocolate
and a magnum of champagne resting in a bucket of ice. Soft
music played in the background. It was the perfect romantic
stage for a dream wedding night.

Beside her, Francesca sighed. "It's stunning. Maybe you
should duck out of the reception and have Gabe come directly up here."

"Tempting." Or it would be if she hadn't seen how grim Gabe appeared when she'd left the reception. "Why don't I get the necklace?"

Kat retrieved the velvet case from the safe and once again spread it on the linen covered table beneath the spotlight of a lamp. She stepped aside so Francesca had an unobstructed view. Endless seconds ticked by.

"Do you have a loupe with you?" Francesca's question sounded tense and riddled with concern.

"No."

"Nor do I." Francesca spared Kat a swift look. "You see it, too, don't you? That's why you asked me to take a look."

"The diamonds…" Her throat had gone so tight, she could barely get the words out. "Some of the stones are fake."

"I won't know for certain until I get a good look at it. But, yes." Francesca touched several of the larger stones. "These aren't fire diamonds. I can say that much definitively. In fact, I seriously doubt they're diamonds, at all."

Kat closed her eyes. How was it possible? And what was she going to do? If the necklace was fake, even partially fake, she'd have to confess all to Gabe. And once she did… "Francesca, I need to know. You of all people will be able to tell if this is—" The words dried up and it took her a moment to gather herself. "I need to know whether any of this is real. Is this even Cara Moretti's necklace?"

Francesca took her time examining the piece, her calm professionalism aiding Kat in recovering her own poise. "I've seen pictures of Heart's Desire." She spoke with authority. "The necklace itself appears genuine. But some of the stones have clearly been replaced. I can't say for certain how many until I have an opportunity to give it a thorough examination."

"I need to know what happened." And even more vitally, "I also need to find out when the stones were sold, if that's possible."

"Absolutely. Try not to panic." She gave Kat a swift hug. "All of our stones are photographed and laser-etched with codes so we can keep track of them. I don't know for certain whether these were encoded, but so few loose fire diamonds ever hit the market, that I can guarantee we'll be able to trace any that have. If the individual stones were removed from the necklace and sold, chances are we can get the pertinent details for you. We might even be able to contact the current owner and buy them back. Then your necklace will be as good as new."

Kat nodded, forcing out a grateful smile. "Thanks." There was only one problem with Francesca's scenario. She couldn't afford to buy back those original diamonds. She didn't even want to consider how much money might be involved. She returned the necklace to its case and handed it to Francesca. "Please call me when you find out what happened."

"Hey, no more worries, okay? Not today of all days." She held out her hand. "Come on. Let's get back to the reception. You have a cake to cut and a wedding night to look forward to."

The rest of the reception passed in a blur. Afterward, Kat had a vague, hazy memory of cutting the cake and feeding a tiny piece to Gabe. She vividly remembered the moment he took her into his arms for the first dance, though. The power of his hold. The feel of his hard, strong body moving against hers. The tenderness of his touch. But when the last note died, it was the kiss he gave her which became forever etched in her memory, a kiss that—if circumstances had been different—might have turned her hope into certainty that their temporary marriage would become a real one.

But how could it? How could he possibly feel anything other than trapped? *She'd* been the one to approach him with this devil's bargain, knowing full well he'd do anything to get his hands on Heart's Desire. *She'd* been the reason he'd gone to the Dantes for help and been forced to openly acknowledge his relationship with them—to admit to the world he was a bastard. And *she'd* been the one to surrender to him, to remain silent about her inexperience. If she'd been more upfront, perhaps he'd have taken better precautions and she wouldn't be...

Pregnant.

If Nonna was right and Kat carried Gabe's baby— granted, a big if—it would change everything, including their relationship. Would he suspect she'd set him up? Would he believe she'd scammed him, especially once he learned the truth about the necklace? She closed her eyes, fighting the panic crashing down on top of her.

"What's wrong?" Gabe's voice slid over and around her, deep and husky, filled with concern. "More bridal jitters?"

"It's all happening so fast." She fought to draw breath. Somehow her gown had shrunk again. "Maybe we should have waited."

"Got it. I think I can solve your problem."

The band slipped seamlessly into another number and Gabe swung her to the edges of the floor and then out through the nearest exit. Wrapping an arm around her waist, he urged her toward the elevators. People they passed smiled indulgently, some calling out good wishes. The car arrived after a few moments and those waiting stepped aside, allowing the newlyweds to make the ride to their suite in privacy.

Kat opened the door with her key card. Before she could step foot across the threshold, Gabe swung her into his arms and carried her into the suite. He took in the setup with a single, all-encompassing glance and headed for the doorway leading to the bedroom. He didn't stop until he reached the bed. Together they took the fall, allowing the soft mattress and even softer duvet to absorb the impact.

Though the curtains were open, sheers muted the light cascading through the windows, leaving the room in soft pastels. He smiled down at her, cupping her cheek and tracing her bottom lip with his thumb. "Have I told you how beautiful you look?"

She managed a smile. "You're looking pretty fine, yourself."

"Okay, that didn't work." His eyes narrowed. "Maybe we should clear the air about a few things. We're in bed. And you know the rules when we are."

Uh-oh. How could she have forgotten? "I'm beginning to hate Bed Honesty," she complained.

"Tough. Time for another honest conversation. Now tell me the truth." His mouth compressed. "Not that I don't already have my suspicions."

Oh, God. He knew. Knew about the necklace. Knew she loved him. Knew she was pregnant and he was trapped with no easy way out. "Gabe—"

Kat stared at Gabe with such a look of panic, he couldn't bring himself to make the moment any worse for her. "You want to work for Dantes," he supplied for her. "Or should I say, you want to work with Francesca. That's why you two went off together."

She blinked in surprise. At a guess, he'd thrown her and it took a second for her to switch gears enough to respond. "With everything that's been going on, we never got around to discussing my career aspirations. I guess I've also been avoiding the subject because—"

"Because you were afraid I'd think you were using my relationship with the Dantes to help you get a job with them," he filled in for her.

"Now that you mention it, I wouldn't be surprised if you thought that. Maybe even suspected I'd planned it from the start."

"Not a chance."

She shook her head. "I don't understand. Why not?"

"Because no one, not even Jessa or Matilda, knew I was Dominic Dante's son. Hell, most of the Dantes didn't know until recently. And I was careful to keep the connection very, very quiet." He lifted an eyebrow. "Unless you somehow found out?"

She met his gaze and answered with absolute sincerity. "I had no idea you were a Dante until you told me. Nor do I want you to ask them for a job on my behalf. If Dantes hires me I want it based on my talents alone."

"Agreed." He paused a beat. "So, we have that cleared up, yes?"

"Yes."

The brevity of her smile warned he'd only uncovered part of the problem. Thank God for Bed Honesty. "But, apparently we haven't cleared everything up. So, what's next?"

"Nonna. Nonna said…" Kat snatched a quick breath, then gave it to him straight. "Nonna said I'm pregnant."

He couldn't help himself. He laughed. "It's been, what? Three days? After only three days, Nonna can tell you're pregnant?"

"It does sound rather ludicrous when you put it that way," Kat admitted. "But everyone says she has the eye."

He brushed her veil back from her face. "I think you've been living in Italy too long."

"Gabe, seriously. What if I am?"

"We discussed this on the plane," he replied with a shrug. "We're married, aren't we?"

"Well, yes."

"If you're pregnant, we'll figure out how best to raise our baby. If that means staying together…" His voice hardened, turned implacable. "Then we stay together. But I won't allow a child of ours to experience what Lucia and I did growing up. Our son or daughter will know both its parents. Clear?"

"It's just that everything's hitting us so fast. We haven't had time to adjust to one issue before another knocks us over. And there's something else." A hint of desperation crept into her voice. "It's about Heart's Desire."

He shook his head, adamant. "Right now I'm not interested in anything but you and me and the fact that this is our wedding night." To his surprise, he discovered it was the absolute truth. Nothing mattered right now, not even his mother's necklace. "Got it?"

"What about five years ago?" she protested.

"Stop." He gave her a slow, impassioned kiss. "I know where you're going with that one and I'd rather you didn't. There won't be anyone in this bed tonight but the two of us. We'll have time to deal with all the other issues tomorrow. But not here. Not now. Just let it go, okay?"

He kissed her again, slowly lifting her to a sitting position, pleased to feel the tension slip from her body and see the worry ease from her brow. So far, Jessa hadn't come between them, at least not in bed. He intended to keep it that way. Whatever had happened the night he'd found Kat in Winters' bed, he hadn't uncovered the full truth. There was something hidden beneath the surface, something that involved his late wife. He'd been so quick to protect Jessa, he hadn't bothered looking deeper at the time. That would have come, he didn't doubt it for a moment. But she'd died two short years into their marriage, when only the first few troubling clouds had appeared on the distant horizon. When suspicion had been no more than a tendril of doubt.

Now the past had collided with the present, taking him in a new direction, one he found far more intriguing than memories from that other life. He dismissed all thought of anyone other than Kat, not the least surprised at the ease with which he did so. How could it be otherwise when he held in his arms the most beautiful woman he'd ever known? She was his wife now. She was the one he was honor bound to protect. And that's just what he'd do.

Gently, he unhooked her wedding gown and eased it from her shoulders. It dropped to her waist, exposing the daintiest bra he'd ever seen, barely more than a wisp of lace. Her skin seemed to glow against the delicate scrap, her breasts filling the cups to overflowing while the skirts of her gown and petticoats mushroomed around her. He found the bra closure and released it. She smiled up at him from where she sat, curled on the bed. She exuded feminine mystery and enchanted allure, looking like a half-naked sea nymph rising from a foaming sea of silk and tulle.

Just as she'd stripped him the night they'd first made love, now it was his turn. He took his time, peeling through her wedding garments, layer by layer, until all that remained was the tulle veil edged in lace. It cascaded over her, softening her nudity and making her all the more bewitching.

"I wish I could take a picture," he murmured.

"Don't you dare. I've had more than enough pictures taken today, thank you."

"None like this."

"You're right. Nor will there be any."

He grinned at her tart response. "I guess I'll have to rely on my memory."

Then his smile faded and he felt the tug of The Inferno, the odd, insistent certainty that he would carry this image of her for the rest of his life, labeled, "My wife on our wedding night." And he sensed there would be other images that would become fixed there. Kat, swollen with his child. Kat, their child nursing at her breast. Kat, tearfully watching their children heading off for their first day of school. Kat, proudly watching those same children graduating. Kat, cradling their first grandchild. Kat, snowy haired and aged, and still the most beautiful woman he'd ever seen. The images formed a kaleidoscope in his head, dizzying in their scope.

Silently, he removed his tux while she watched, her lovely eyes the same shade as new growth. A new beginning. He shed the last of his clothes and came down beside her, parting the edges of the veil that separated her from him. Where before he'd seen possibilities—a misty future stretching before them—now he saw only this woman and this instant of his life, the moment finely honed. He steeped himself in it, absorbing it, relishing every second, every small step and subtle tick of the clock.

The first time he'd made love to her there had been a newness to their touch, laden with a hint of uncertainty. When he took her in his arms this time, it was with a man's knowledge of how best to satisfy his woman. He'd already discovered some of her endless secrets, just as she had discovered his. It brought a deeper intimacy to each caress. To the slow, drugged kisses. To those places known only to him which would bring her the greatest pleasure.

"Gabe…" Kat smiled against his skin, touching his flat, male nipples with the tip of her tongue and threatening to send him straight over the edge. "I know what I want this time."

He released a groan that was half laugh. "Tell me it's the same thing you wanted last time."

She smiled her woman's smile, the one that caused The Inferno to pound and burn and demand. "That, too. But I also want…" Her lips drifted close to his ear and she whispered a suggestion, one that took his breath away. "Can we try that?"

"Everything. Everything and anything," he promised.

"It might take a while."

"We have all night. Hell, we have all of tomorrow, if that's what it takes to satisfy you."

"I think it just might."

They spent the entire next day in bed, rarely far from each other's arms. It was a time apart, a time where two became one. In body. In heart. In soul.

Sometimes they came together in humor, as they had the first time they made love. Other occasions, Gabe made love to his wife with heartbreaking urgency, as though desperate to cling to their rapidly dwindling time together, time which slipped by like raindrops through cupped fingers. They both sensed something looming on the horizon, a consequence to their changing the terms of their contract before the issues between them had been resolved.

The last time they came together, was in the deepest part of the night, when ghosts lurked in the shadows and the heavy silence spoke volumes. Kat clung to him, shuddering beneath his touch, the air so saturated with desire he could practically taste it. Instead, he tasted her. She was beyond sweet, beyond spicy. It was as though someone had discovered the perfect flavor, one made specifically for him and only him. And that flavor was Kat.

He cupped her breasts, finding the most delicious of nectars beneath his tongue. The catch of her breath and the pounding of her heart gave a voice to her taste. His hands skated lower and now he could feel her flavor, as well as hear and taste it. Feel the honey of her skin, how it flowed beneath his fingertips, rippling and undulating. And then he reached the core of her, where sweetness mingled with spice. The very center of what made her a woman, the full-bodied richness that belonged to his wife and only his wife.

And he consumed her, lost himself where all their senses joined. Came alive. Began and ended and began again. Her cries of release shattered the darkness, sent the shadows fleeing and turned night into something dazzling and radiant. And then he took her again, melding their bodies, mating them in a moment so perfect it would always live inside him.

Even when it finished, it didn't end. She turned to him, still part of him in sleep, her body mated with his, his essence still warm within her body. Words hovered on the tip of his tongue, words he longed to speak but had never given voice to. Almost he said them. But they wouldn't form. It was as though some final barrier held them fast. But that didn't change the fact that he knew. Knew what he felt for Kat. Knew it was real and permanent and forever.

Gently, ever so gently, he took her hand and curled it into a fist. And then he linked her index finger with his and let his heart speak the words that wouldn't become.

Gabe, Kat and Matilda returned to Seattle the next day. Based on the vague air of apprehension that seemed to descend the farther they distanced themselves from San Francisco, he suspected she felt exactly the same way he did. She was waiting for the shoe to drop, waiting for the fairy tale to shatter and for reality to intrude on what had been a beautiful interlude, but one that couldn't last.

Of course, he didn't expect his own sister to be the one to drop that shoe, or for it to be two days before Christmas.

Gabe's private line rang and he picked it up automatically, pausing just long enough to make a notation on the contract in front of him before speaking. "Moretti."

"Gabe?" Tension rippled through his sister's voice. "Are you there?"

He came instantly alert. "Lucia? What's wrong?" Because something was definitely wrong.

"I just heard something about Mom's necklace." She paused, as though bracing herself. "Were you aware the Dantes have it?"

That stopped him cold. "Wait. Wait one damn minute. How the *hell* did they end up with it?"

"Kat gave it to Francesca the day you were married." A long sigh came through the phone. "I gather from your re-action you didn't know."

"No, I damn well didn't know. I didn't even know Kat had it on her." Though now that he thought about it, she'd mentioned something about the necklace on their wedding night. Had that been what she'd wanted to tell him? "Why the hell didn't she give it to me?"

Another long, uncomfortable pause. "Maybe because the necklace is a fake," Lucia admitted. "At least, that's what the Dantes are claiming."

Gabe felt himself turn as cold and icy as the snow spit-ting earthward outside his window. "A fake," he repeated.

"Okay, maybe not a fake exactly. But Francesca said some of the diamonds aren't real."

"They were sure as hell real when I sold it to Matilda. We had it appraised."

"Well, they're not—anymore. Listen, they've put a pri-vate detective named Juice on the case. From what I've heard about him, he'll get to the bottom of it."

"Did Kat know it was a fake when she turned it over to them?" He shoved the question out through gritted teeth. When his sister didn't immediately respond, he pushed harder. "Answer me, damn it. Did she realize it was a fake when she gave it to them?"

"I'm sorry, Gabe. Yes, she knew." Lucia hesitated before asking, "What are you going to do?" Apprehension riddled her question.

"Get to the bottom of it from my end."

"Don't hurt her!"

"I'm not going to hurt her," he snapped. Reconsidered. "Much."

Gabe hung up without another word. Shoving back his chair, he crossed to the bank of windows and stared out at the sprawl of buildings through the curtain of pelting snow. Damn, damn, *damn*. He'd come so close. So incredibly close. For the first time in memory, he'd trusted someone, unconditionally. Had bought into the fairy tale he'd always cautioned Lucia to resist.

It was those eyes. Those sweet, innocent eyes, as dewy and unspoiled as spring leaves. She seemed so genuine. So sincere. Appeared to succumb utterly to The Inferno. Even worse, she'd been wounded, much as he had, sharing his wariness, his inability to trust. And yet, the two of them had trusted. Despite all that stood between them, they'd given themselves, heart and soul, to one another.

Fool. Idiot. She was conning him. And instead of seeing through the con as he'd normally have done, he'd been led right into her trap by parts of him that had no business making any decision other than how often and how long. He should have demanded to see the necklace. Had it examined by an expert. How could someone with his experience have neglected to follow the most basic of business procedures?

Because he'd wanted to believe. He'd wanted Kat, even rushing her into marriage. Well, now he had her. The real question was...

What the hell did he plan to do with her?

Christmas lights flickered up at him from the street below, twinkling gaily, symbolizing a deep-seeded belief, filled with profound meaning. One that encouraged faith and hope and peace. He rested the palm of his hand against the glass, felt the stirring of The Inferno, felt the throbbing pulse of the powerful connection he'd forged with Kat. And he heard a small voice, at the core of his being, insisting he was wrong. Insisting there had to be a rational explanation.

A voice that insisted he trust the woman he loved.

He closed his eyes and fought the pain and disillusionment that had shaped his life into one of caution and distrust. And he realized he had a choice. He could trust—against all odds—and move forward. Or he could take a step back and return to the safety of his world before Kat had swept into it.

He opened his eyes and made his decision.

Ten

Kat's cell phone rang and she retrieved it from her pocket, her gloves making her fumble a bit. She yanked them off and stuffed them in her pocket, glancing at the display. Francesca's name flashed and she felt her nerves stretch taut. "Merry Christmas!" she said, hope warring with dread. "Are you all set for the big day?"

"Almost." Francesca's voice matched hers—one attempting to conceal her distress beneath a bright, shiny wrapping of enthusiasm topped with a pretty little bow of forced cheerfulness. "Just one or two last minute gifts to wrap and…" Her breath exploded in a sigh. "Oh, Kat. I'm so sorry. But it's bad news. Not all bad, but definitely not good."

Kat kept moving, lifting her coat collar against the spate of snow swirling down from a leaden sky. For some reason it became more of an effort to put one foot in front of another. "How bad?"

"I'll give it to you straight. You were right. Some of the

stones are fake. But here's the good news. The necklace, it-self, is genuine. So are most of the stones."

"How many are fakes?"

"Six." A significant pause. "The largest six, I'm afraid."

Six? So many! Kat fought to speak coherently, to form even the simplest of sentences. "Have you been able to track the stones?"

"We have. There won't be any problem at all restoring the necklace." Francesca's voice took on a soothing quality. But it ended up having just the opposite effect. "Primo's mak-ing arrangements to buy the diamonds back as we speak."

Dollar signs flashed before Kat's eyes. "For how much?" The question came out low and thready. She cleared her throat. "I know you can't give me an exact figure. But ball-park."

The figure had her knees threatening to give out. She stumbled to a stop in front of a department store window, decked out for Christmas. She stared at the scene, some tiny portion of her brain still functioning enough to take it in. Fake snow rained down over a storybook setting, com-plete with a traditionally decorated tree and a toy train mer-rily steaming along its track. Overhead, snowflakes swirled earthward, mirroring the scene in the window. They hit her exposed skin and she shivered at their icy touch. The fore-cast called for a white Christmas. It seemed they were about to be proven right.

"Kat? Kat are you still there?"

"Yes, Francesca. Thank you for letting me know. Keep me updated, will you?"

Something in Kat's voice must have given her away. "Try not to worry," Francesca urged. "I'm sure Primo will work something out with Gabe."

"No. No, this is my problem. *I'll* work it out with Gabe."

"If you say so. Have a good Christmas," she said gently.

"You, too."

Kat spared the window a wistful glance, longing for the dream it represented. No wonder her grandmother hadn't wanted to sell Gabe the necklace. How could she when she'd sold off a number of the diamonds. But why? Because of her illness? Or had she lost her money sometime over the past few years when the economy had gone south? What had compelled her to sell some of the diamonds? And why not approach Gabe and sell the necklace to him, intact? He'd have paid whatever she'd asked. He'd made no bones about that.

There was only one way to know for certain, not that it would change anything. She should have told Gabe about her suspicions. Told him before they ever married that she suspected the diamonds in Heart's Desire had been replaced. By not doing so, it made her look very, very guilty. Would it be the final straw for him? Would her silence make it impossible for him to trust her? She hit a hot button on her phone, the one she'd designated for Gabe. He answered immediately, almost as though he'd been expecting her call.

"Is there any chance you can cut out early and meet me at my grandmother's?"

"I think so. Problem?"

She sighed. "I'm not sure, yet. I'm on my way over there now."

He didn't waste time on idle chitchat. "Be there in twenty."

Kat pocketed her phone. Snow drifted down around her, a bit heavier than it had been just five minutes before. Even though it was only midafternoon, the curtain of snow made it appear much later, muffling sound. She stared at the window display, seeing her ghostly reflection mirrored there, as well as the cityscape behind her. For an instant, it felt as though she were enclosed in a soft globe that held time at bay, locking her between two worlds—the life she'd led before Jessa had chosen to destroy her world, and the one she'd built with Gabe. Now those two worlds were colliding, the old shattering the new, and she was helpless to prevent it from happening…unless a miracle occurred.

For some reason, despite all odds, a tendril of optimism took root. It was the season for miracles, wasn't it? Maybe, just maybe, she could still straighten everything out. Maybe, just maybe, she wouldn't lose Gabe in the process.

The reflection from Christmas lights flickered in the window, twinkling gaily, symbolizing a deep-seeded belief, filled with profound meaning. One that encouraged faith and hope and peace. Kat rested the palm of her hand against the glass of the window display and felt the stirring of The Inferno, felt the throbbing pulse of the powerful connection she'd forged with Gabe. And she heard a small voice, at the very core of her being, urging her to go to him. Tell him everything.

A voice that insisted she fully open herself to the man she loved.

She closed her eyes and fought the fear that had shaped the past five years into ones of caution and distrust. And she realized she had a choice. She could put her trust in Gabe and move forward. Or she could take a step back and return to the safety of her world before he'd first touched her.

She opened her eyes and made her decision, turning resolutely toward her Heart's Desire.

Gabe swept into Matilda's parlor like an avenging angel, his black snow-dusted coat swirling around him. One look at his expression and Kat's prayer for a Christmas miracle died an early death. She didn't know how or when, but he'd heard about Heart's Desire. And there wasn't a doubt in her mind that his discovery spelled a fast and painful end to their marriage.

She released her grandmother's hand and stood. "Gabe…"

His gaze rested for a brief instant on Matilda, before snapping in her direction. He stared at her, his golden eyes tarnished into darkness. "I believe you have something to tell me."

She nodded, unable to look away, trapped within that fierce bleakness. "First, you should know that I gave Francesca your mother's necklace to examine."

"When?"

She flinched at that single, biting word. "The day we were married."

"Why?"

She spared her grandmother a brief, anguished glance. "Gam gave me Heart's Desire the morning of our wedding and suggested I surprise you by wearing it."

"But you didn't wear it." His smile reflected the wintry coldness outside. "I would have noticed if you had."

She swallowed—hard—and gave it to him straight. "Some of the stones didn't look right to me, so I told Gam that, given its history, wearing it in front of all the Dantes might not be the most diplomatic option."

"Clever." It didn't sound like a compliment.

"I then asked Francesca to examine the necklace during our wedding reception. She…she agreed with me. Several of the stones weren't fire diamonds."

"Do you mean to say, Heart's Desire is a fake?" Matilda demanded in a shocked voice. "That isn't possible."

"The necklace, itself, isn't a fake," Kat hastened to reassure. She crouched beside her grandmother's chair, relieved to finally escape her husband's implacable gaze. "But some of the diamonds aren't real."

"They were real when I sold the necklace to your grandmother," Gabe stated, folding his arms across his chest. "It was certified by an expert. So, if there's a problem now, it's happened since the sale."

"And I'm telling you that's simply not possible," Matilda protested. "Other than to have the necklace cleaned and re-appraised a few years back, I haven't touched it."

Kat twisted her hands together and frowned. The engagement ring Gabe had given her during the reception bit into her skin, the sharp pain a tiny reflection of what she'd soon face when her marriage ended. Why didn't her grandmother simply admit the truth? After all, it was her necklace. If she chose to sell off bits and pieces of it, that was her prerogative.

"Gam… You must know that six of the diamonds have been replaced."

Gabe stepped forward, shrugging off his coat and tossing it over the arm of a nearby chair. "But you don't know, do you, Matilda?"

She shook her head without speaking, pressing her trembling lips tightly together.

Kat rocked back on her heels, and stared at her grandmother, stunned. "Wait a minute. I assumed— But, if you didn't sell off any of the diamonds, then who…?"

"There are—*were*—three logical possibilities," Gabe replied. "I also assumed Matilda was responsible, which would have explained her reluctance to sell me the necklace these past few years. There are two problems with that scenario."

Matilda lifted her chin in a proud gesture. "Which are?"

"Why sell off the diamonds one by one, when you knew I'd have paid you a bloody fortune for the thing?" His rationale echoed Kat's.

"And the other reason?"

He smiled with surprising kindness. "I only have to look at you to know your shock isn't faked. You really didn't know there was anything wrong with the necklace. If you had, you wouldn't have dared give it to your granddaughter to wear at our wedding. It would have been far too risky with so many experts around, any one of whom would have spotted the fake diamonds."

Kat slowly stood to face her husband. "You said three scenarios. If it wasn't Matilda, then who else?" A bitter chill settled over her. "Me, I assume."

"Oh, definitely you, my love."

Matilda stiffened. "Gabe, no. She couldn't have—"

He spared Kat's grandmother a look of regret. "The only other possibility is Jessa. Those are the only other logical options." His returned his gaze to his wife while continuing to address Matilda. "You told me Kat loved Heart's Desire. That it helped shape who and what she's become. Maybe it helped her more than you realize."

"Is that what you truly believe?" Kat demanded.

"Tell me, my dear wife. How did you support yourself in Italy? How have you been able to afford designer clothes and footwear? Maybe when you realized you were going to lose everything to Jessa you decided to help yourself to a few of the choicer stones. Such perfect symmetry, isn't it? Using the fire diamonds to pay for your training in jewelry design? Selling them off one at a time in order to finance your education. To pay for your daily expenses, along with a few luxuries you couldn't live without, like those sexy little shoes you're currently wearing."

"I worked for everything I own," she snapped, bristling with defiance. "I worked three jobs at times, every day, all day, without any outside help. Everything I've accomplished in the past five years, I've done on my own."

"If you say so."

"I say so."

He lifted a shoulder in a noncommittal shrug. "Then we'll move on to option number three. Jessa."

Her name hung in the air between them. Matilda seemed to shrink in on herself. "Jessa?" she asked fretfully.

"It's the only other logical option. No one else had access to the necklace, did they?"

Matilda shook her head. "No," she whispered.

"Then it's either Kat or Jessa, and I don't think there's much question about who it is." He allowed the words to settle before continuing. "After all, it was Kat who attempted to seduce Benson Winters. Kat who betrayed her cousin. Kat who adored Heart's Desire. Kat who couldn't stand the idea of it going to Jessa."

"Stop it, Gabe." Kat stepped between him and her grandmother. "Leave her alone. If you want to come after me one-on-one, fine. I'm ready for you. But not Gam. I won't let you hurt her."

"I'm just trying to get your grandmother to consider the situation logically. For her to figure out what I already know."

"And what do you know?" she demanded, fighting tears. "Or rather, what do you *think* you know?"

He tilted his head to one side. "Surprisingly, there's very little thought involved. I suppose that's why it took me so long to understand."

Kat stared at him, utterly confused. "Okay, now you've lost me."

"I hope not."

Then he looked at her. Just a simple look. For an instant she couldn't bring herself to interpret that look—like Gabe—found it difficult to align logic and reason with what her heart was telling her. He was saying something to her. Something she didn't understand, but which caused her palm to throb in response. She rubbed at the burning itch, felt the heat of The Inferno flare to life. She hesitated, her hand slipping to cup her abdomen, cradling the spark of life she suspected lived beneath her palm. And that's when certainty swept through her.

She didn't know why he was painting her with the guilt brush. She simply knew that he didn't believe it for one little minute. He continued to regard her with an implacable expression and she realized he had no intention of explaining. No intention of reassuring her. She either trusted him or she didn't. She made him wait an endless thirty seconds. Mean of her, true. But hey, he'd given her a few queasy minutes, too.

She stepped closer to him, until they stood no more than a foot apart. She still held her hand over her abdomen, over the baby sleeping there, and she slowly formed a fist. And then she crooked her index finger.

His eyes closed for a split second and she literally felt the tension break over him like a tidal wave, before dissolving. Ever so gently, his hand formed a matching fist and he linked fingers with her. The Inferno pulsed between them, sweeping through her veins like the sweetest of wines.

"I'll reimburse you for the diamonds," Matilda said quietly. "But only if you agree this matter ends here."

Kat returned to her grandmother's side and gave her arthritic hands a gentle, reassuring squeeze. "It's all right, Gam."

"No, it's not all right," Gabe retorted. "Either you are guilty or Jessa is. I want Matilda to tell me which one it is. I think she knows. I think deep down she realizes that she made a horrible mistake five years ago. That's why she asked you to come home. And that's why she claimed she was dying."

"I am dying," Matilda retorted. Then she ruffled the air with a sweep of her hand. "I may have exaggerated how soon that might happen. But as I told you. Life is a terminal condition and I'm a good piece closer to the end of that life than to its start."

"Oh, Gam, why?" Kat asked, shaken. "Why would you do such a thing? Do you have any idea how frantic I've been at the idea of losing you?"

Tears gathered in Matilda's eyes. One escaped, running along a deep rivulet time had carved into her face. "I was afraid you wouldn't return unless you thought I was dying. Even then, I wasn't entirely sure you would come."

Kat gathered her grandmother up in a tight hug. "Don't be ridiculous. Of course, I came back. I love you. You're all the family I have left. Why do you think I've continued to write to you all these years?"

Matilda's chin quivered for an instant before she regained control. She shot Gabe a hard, direct look. "Kat would never have done anything to Heart's Desire. Never. She cherished that necklace, thought it was the most beautiful thing she'd ever seen. She'd sooner cut off her arm than do anything that would devalue it."

He closed his eyes, understanding crashing down on him. "That's why you refused to sell it to me all these years, isn't it? Because Kat loved it so much."

She nodded, more tears tracking down her cheeks. "It was my last connection to her."

"And Jessa?" he asked quietly.

Matilda sighed. "She came to see me the day she died. She was furious because I'd told her I still intended to give the necklace to Kat. I wondered…" She bowed her head. "I wondered if she thought by marrying you, I'd eventually change my mind and leave it to her."

Gabe appeared startled. "I never expected you to give it away. I always hoped to buy it from you."

She waved that aside. "Jessa had other plans." She hesitated, guilt settling like a shadow on her face. "I have a confession to make about the day she died. I…I've always blamed myself for her death. Maybe if we hadn't fought about the necklace, she wouldn't have driven so recklessly."

Gabe refused to let her get away with it. "It was her choice. Her decision to drive the way she did. And she paid the ultimate price for that decision."

It was then Kat realized he no longer retained any protective feelings toward Jessa. That somehow, at some point, he'd stopped believing in her…and started believing in Kat. That whatever love he'd felt for his first wife had evaporated, his allegiance transferring, for good. Light caught the fire diamond gracing her engagement ring and released the inner flames. They burst free in an arc of brilliant color, as though confirming her prayer that maybe…just maybe, she'd been given a Christmas miracle, after all.

She must have made some sound because he spared her a questioning glance before continuing. "But I can tell you with absolute certainty that Jessa sold the diamonds."

Kat started. "How do you know?"

"I called Primo on my way here. Asked when the stones were sold and if they could identify the seller. There's no question it was her."

Matilda's mouth dropped open. "You knew that when you walked in here?"

Gabe nodded. "But I needed you to figure it out for yourself, to realize Kat was the innocent one."

"Well, I can't say I approve of your methods," she informed him sharply, "though I will admit they're effective."

"I apologize, but it seemed the most expedient way to force everything out into the open." He approached and leaned in, planted a kiss on her wrinkled cheek. "If you don't mind, I'd like to take my wife home. I guarantee I owe her an apology as well."

"Count on it," Kat muttered.

He spared her a swift smile before returning his attention to Matilda. "Since tomorrow's Christmas Eve, why don't we swing by and pick you up? You can stay at our place for the night and celebrate Christmas Day with us."

Matilda returned his smile with a tremulous one of her own. "Thank you. I'd like that."

"And don't worry about the diamonds. All you have to do at this point is stay healthy. Kat would like her grandmother around for a nice long time." He gave her a naughty wink and whispered, "Long enough to become a great-grand-mother a few times over."

The drive to Medina took twice as long due to the weather. As far as Kat was concerned, it felt endless, especially since she and Gabe had a number of issues still to resolve, none of which she cared to discuss in the car while creeping across Evergreen Point. By the time they arrived home, night had descended and the house and grounds were covered in a soft blanket of white. They entered the silent house and he led the way to the study. It created an odd symmetry to create a final resolution here, mere steps from where they'd first discovered their Inferno connection.

The room was lit by firelight from the stone fireplace. In the bay window a Christmas tree twinkled gaily, the roman-tic setting no doubt courtesy of Gabe's housekeeper Dennis before he'd left for the evening. Gabe grabbed some cushions from the sofa and tossed them onto the floor in front of the tree so they could watch the fire while they talked. Drawing Kat down beside him, he wrapped his arms around her and pulled her close. Cupping her face, he leaned in and kissed her. She reached for him, clung to him.

Several long minutes passed in passionate silence before Gabe pulled back slightly and stared down at her. "Truth time."

"Bed Honesty?"

He shrugged. "Considering I plan on making love to you here, I think this qualifies as a bed for our purposes." He smoothed her hair back from her face. "Tell me about Jessa so we can finally close that door."

"Some of it's speculation, and some of it's based on what Benson told me," she warned. "He called a couple of days ago to apologize for misjudging me. He said it took him a little while, but he finally realized I'd been set up as much as he had."

"Still, I'd like to hear your version of what happened."

She sighed. "You have to know that Jessa and I didn't enjoy a very close relationship. Some of it was our age difference. Some of it was her resentment over the bond I shared with Gam. Whatever the reason, Jessa and I were cordial… but distant. And then Benson happened."

"I know she met Winters when she worked on his campaign."

"Yes. They released the news about their engagement right after he announced his candidacy. His numbers experienced a nice bump as a result. It began to look like he had a real shot at winning."

Gabe's brows pulled together. "So what went wrong? The tell-all his ex wrote didn't come out until after the scandal with you broke."

"I asked Benson about that," she confessed. "He said his campaign manager received advance notice that the tell-all was coming and warned Jessa. Said the book would put his ability to win in serious jeopardy. He claimed she didn't take it well."

"You think she decided it was time to cut her losses and move on?"

Kat nodded. "It would explain a lot. A week later she called me, said she wanted to create a closer relationship, wanted us to be more like sisters than cousins, especially

since we didn't have any family other than Gam. She suggested a girl's night. She rented a suite so we could have
dinner, wine, massages."

"Even though you were underage?"

She winced. "Well...yeah. I think that was probably part
of the appeal. The naughtiness of it all. Remember, I was
raised by a very strict grandmother." She closed her eyes,
the dispassion in her voice at odds with the pain ripping
through her. "Like a fool, I went," she whispered.

Gabe tightened his arms around her. "It's over. It can't
hurt you anymore." He feathered a kiss across her brow. "I
assume Jessa drugged you? And arranged for Benson to
drop by?"

She nodded, shuddered. "I woke up to find myself in
bed, naked. You were there. Benson was there." Her chin
trembled, and she took a moment to gather her self-possession. "And the media showed up almost immediately after."

Gabe closed his eyes. "The things I said... I can't apologize enough. Jessa told me you'd always been jealous of
her, had set out to seduce her fiancé. I believed her, was so
certain she was the wronged party." He rested his cheek
against the top of her head. "And instead, she'd decided
Winters was on his way down and this was her clever way
of bailing before that happened."

"She couldn't just dump him. It would have made her
look bad. Plus, she already had her sights on a replacement
for Benson. You were making quite a splash by then, very
much on the way up. And she played on your protective instincts by painting herself in the role of the victim."

"Why use you?"

"Because I was young and foolish enough not to question her motives," she admitted with gut-wrenching honesty.
"And because I stood between her and Gam, or rather Gam's
money. And more important, Heart's Desire."

He lifted her chin and forced her to look at him. Tears filled her eyes, tears she desperately attempted to control. "You can say it, Kat," he told her gently. "You can finally say the words. And this time, someone will believe you."

The tears escaped, sliding down her cheeks. It took three tries before she managed to push out the words. "I didn't do it." She closed her eyes and surrendered to the tears. To lance a wound which had tormented her for five long years. To finally release all the pain and bitterness. "I didn't do it. I'm innocent."

He simply held her while she cried it out. Held her as though he'd never let her go. When the tears finally ended, he wiped her face, nodding in satisfaction. "Much better."

And miraculously, it was. "One problem resolved?" she asked with a watery smile.

"It was never a problem, just a question I needed answered so we could start our marriage with a clean slate, without the ghost of Jessa hanging over us. I can't apologize enough for my part in what happened all those years ago, Kat. For not realizing Jessa set you up."

"You weren't to know. She was always good at manipulating people."

"Shall we move on to the next issue?" He reached above her head and nudged a pretty golden bell with his finger. Its bright peal silvered the air, reminding her of the bells that had sounded on their wedding day. "Why didn't you tell me when you first suspected something was wrong with the necklace?"

She shrugged. "It was only a few hours before the ceremony and your family arrived within minutes of my discovery. They were all quick to inform me that Primo had confiscated your phone so I had no way to contact you. Besides, I hoped I was mistaken about the necklace." Her brows drew together. "Not that I was."

"When did you know for sure?"

"When I brought Francesca to our suite after the wedding." She glanced hesitantly at him. "You were talking to Primo, remember?"

"Vividly."

"She pretty much confirmed my suspicions." Kat shifted restlessly. "Maybe I should have stopped the ceremony and discussed the problem with you. I certainly considered it."

"I think what you were actually considering, was running."

She laughed, the sound husky from her crying jag. "True." She gazed at him uncertainly. "So what do we do now? You married me so you could finally get your hands on the necklace. Everything that's happened instead isn't at all what you bargained for."

"True." He cupped her cheek, stroking his thumb just beneath her bottom lip. "And I'm afraid our original deal can't be fully consummated until you've replaced the diamonds."

"Do you have any idea what they're worth?" she protested. "I'll never be able to afford to replace them."

She couldn't read his reaction. Once again, his expression turned impassive. "In fact, I'm counting on it."

She shook her head. "I don't understand."

"I figure it'll take you, oh, fifty or sixty years to pay off what you owe me for those diamonds."

A tendril of hope speared through her, a brilliant lightness and joy. "You think I can do it that soon?"

He shrugged. "Probably not, especially if I tack on interest."

"So, I'm stuck with you?"

He smiled down at her. Where before she'd been unable to catch any inkling of his innermost thoughts, now she saw a wealth of love and tenderness. "I'm afraid there's no choice. You are stuck with me. At least until the deal is fully consummated."

"In fifty or sixty years?"

"As you said, probably longer."

Slowly, she formed a fist with her hand, curling her index finger. He mimicked the gesture, linked their fingers together. "I love you, Gabe Moretti," she whispered.

"I love you, too, Kat Moretti. I think I have from the moment we first touched. I know I have since the moment I made love to you." He feathered a kiss across her mouth. "Do you agree to my demands?"

Her eyes fluttered closed and she pursued the kiss, deepened it. "Without question."

He pulled back a tantalizing few inches and offered a teasing smile. "Now for our final problem."

"Which is?"

He cupped her abdomen. "What to name our baby."

She slid her hand on top of his, this time linking all their fingers. "You really think I'm pregnant?"

"According to the Dantes, there's a very real possibility."

"So what do you want to name him? Nonna said it was a boy," she hastened to add.

Gabe hesitated, abruptly serious. Very serious. "Primo made a suggestion on our wedding day."

It only took her a moment to make the connection. "That conversation you had when Francesca and I went upstairs?"

"Yes."

"What name did he want us to consider?"

"Dante." For an instant Gabe's voice failed him. "Only, he wasn't suggesting it for a first name, but for a last. He asked if I'd consider taking his name, either by legally changing it or through adoption."

"Oh, Gabe." Her heart broke for him. She knew at one

point in his life, he'd have given anything for his father to have done that for him. "What did you say?"

The sun rose in his eyes, turning them a shattering gold. Before, a shadow had always tarnished their brilliance. But no longer. He gathered her hand in his so their palms bumped together, then melded, Inferno against Inferno. Heat rushed through them, a sweetness and joy that eclipsed all that had led them to this moment.

"Assuming you have no objections," Gabe replied. "I said we'd be honored to become Dantes."

"You won't become a Dante just because you change your name." She drew him down for another slow, thorough kiss. "You were born a Dante, Gabe. You always have been and you always will be. Just as you always have been and always will be my Inferno mate."

He pulled her close and held on tight. "Just as you always have been and always will be my Heart's Desire."

The snow fell outside their window, a blanket of purity surrounding a heart of warmth. Christmas had arrived early. And its gift was the return of faith and unwavering trust. It had led them to each other. To a family they'd always longed to know. To a bright and shining future with the promise of a son. A son who'd experience his Dante legacy and bear the name Dante from the day of his birth.

It had started as a faint, wavering spark, one that had caught, held, becoming an Inferno. But at its heart of hearts, becoming something far more.

Becoming Dante.

* * * * *

REQUEST YOUR FREE BOOKS!
2 FREE NOVELS PLUS 2 FREE GIFTS!

ALWAYS POWERFUL, PASSIONATE AND PROVOCATIVE

YES! Please send me 2 FREE Harlequin Desire® novels and my 2 FREE gifts (gifts are worth about $10). After receiving them, if I don't wish to receive any more books, I can return the shipping statement marked "cancel." If I don't cancel, I will receive 6 brand-new novels every month and be billed just $4.30 per book in the U.S. or $4.99 per book in Canada. That's a saving of at least 14% off the cover price! It's quite a bargain! Shipping and handling is just 50¢ per book in the U.S. and 75¢ per book in Canada.* I understand that accepting the 2 free books and gifts places me under no obligation to buy anything. I can always return a shipment and cancel at any time. Even if I never buy another book, the two free books and gifts are mine to keep forever.

225/326 HDN FEF3

Name _____ (PLEASE PRINT)

Address _____ Apt. #

City _____ State/Prov. _____ Zip/Postal Code

Signature (if under 18, a parent or guardian must sign)

Mail to the **Reader Service:**
IN U.S.A.: P.O. Box 1867, Buffalo, NY 14240-1867
IN CANADA: P.O. Box 609, Fort Erie, Ontario L2A 5X3

Not valid for current subscribers to Harlequin Desire books.

Want to try two free books from another line?
Call 1-800-873-8635 or visit www.ReaderService.com.

* Terms and prices subject to change without notice. Prices do not include applicable taxes. Sales tax applicable in N.Y. Canadian residents will be charged applicable taxes. Offer not valid in Quebec. This offer is limited to one order per household. All orders subject to credit approval. Credit or debit balances in a customer's account(s) may be offset by any other outstanding balance owed by or to the customer. Please allow 4 to 6 weeks for delivery. Offer available while quantities last.

Your Privacy—The Reader Service is committed to protecting your privacy. Our Privacy Policy is available online at www.ReaderService.com or upon request from the Reader Service.

We make a portion of our mailing list available to reputable third parties that offer products we believe may interest you. If you prefer that we not exchange your name with third parties, or if you wish to clarify or modify your communication preferences, please visit us at www.ReaderService.com/consumerschoice or write to us at Reader Service Preference Service, P.O. Box 9062, Buffalo, NY 14269. Include your complete name and address.

HDES11B

Dial up the passion to Red-Hot with the Harlequin Blaze series!

Harlequin Blaze stories sizzle with strong heroines and irresistible heroes playing the game of modern love and lust. They're fun, sexy and always steamy.

HARLEQUIN®

Blaze

Red-Hot Reads

www.Harlequin.com

HBPOST

SPECIAL EXCERPT FROM HARLEQUIN® BLAZE™

Bestselling Blaze author Jo Leigh
delivers a sizzling *The Wrong Bed* story with

Lying in Bed

Ryan woke to the bed dipping. For a few seconds, his adrenaline spiked until he remembered where he was. He groaned at the bright red numbers on the clock. "One a.m.? What…?"

The rest of the question got lost in the dark, but it didn't matter, because Jeannie didn't answer. His fellow agent on this sting must be exhausted after arriving late. "You okay?"

She tugged sharply on the covers, pulling more of them to her side of the bed.

Ryan could just make out her head on the pillow, her back to him, hunched and tight. Must have gotten stuck at the airport….

He curled onto his side, hoping to find the dream she'd interrupted. It had been nice. Smelled nice. He sighed as he let himself slip deeper and deeper into sleep…. The scent came back, a little like the beach and jasmine, low-key and sexy—

His eyes flew open. His heart thudded as his pulse raced. No need to panic. That was Jeannie next to him. Who else would it be?

Undercover jitters. It happened. Not to him, but he'd heard tales. Moving slowly, Ryan twisted until he could see his bed partner.

He swallowed as his gaze went to the back of Jeannie's head. Was it the moonlight? Jeannie's blond hair looked darker. And

HBEXP1212JLREV

longer. He moved closer, took a deep breath.

"What the—" Ryan sat up so fast the whole bed shook. His hand flailed in his search for the light switch.

It wasn't Jeannie next to him. Jeannie smelled like baby powder and bananas. The woman next to him smelled exactly like...

She groaned, and as she turned over, he whispered, "No, no, no, no."

Special Agent Angie Wolf glared back at him with red-rimmed eyes.

"Jeannie is being held over in court," she snapped. "I'd rather not be here, but we don't have much choice if we want to salvage the operation."

She punched the pillow, looked once more in his direction and said, "Oh, and if you wake me before eight, I'll kill you with my bare hands," then pulled the covers over her head.

No way could Ryan pretend to be married to Angie Wolf. This operation was possible because Jeannie and he were buddies. Hell, he was pals with her husband and played with her kids.

Angie Wolf was another story. She was hot, for one thing. Hot as in smokin' hot. Tall, curvy and those legs...

God, just a few hours ago, he'd been laughing about the Intimate at Last brochure. Body work. Couples massages. *Delightful homeplay assignments.* How was this supposed to work now?

Ryan stared into the darkness. Angie Wolf was going to be his wife. For a week. Holy hell.

Pick up LYING IN BED by Jo Leigh.
On sale December 18, 2012, from Harlequin Blaze.